"Whether you like it or not, I intend to follow you home."

Aaron's tone was severe. "After spending the evening sorting you out, I might as well finish the job."

"Sorting— Finish the... But you weren't even going to Cinnamon Bay," protested Emily.

"Actually I wasn't going anywhere in particular. I'm just exploring Vancouver Island. One stop is as good as another."

"Stop?" Emily heard the squeak in her voice, and made an effort to control it. "What do you mean, stop?"

Aaron pointed the flashlight at his watch. "In case you haven't noticed, it's late, and my daughter's sleeping in the car. I'm prepared to escort you home, but I'm not planning on traveling any farther."

"Wait. You can't stay with me," objected Emily. "I'm grateful for your help, but—"

"But you're not about to spend the night with the Big Bad Wolf," he interrupted dryly.

Kay Gregory grew up in England, but moved to Canada as a teenager. She now lives in Vancouver with her husband, two sons, one dog and two ferrets. She has had innumerable jobs, some interesting, some extremely boring, which have often provided background for her books. Now that she is writing Harlequin romance novels, Kay thinks she has at last found a job that she won't find necessary to change.

Books by Kay Gregory

HARLEQUIN ROMANCE

3016—A PERFECT BEAST
3058—IMPULSIVE BUTTERFLY
3082—AMBER AND AMETHYST
3152—YESTERDAY'S WEDDING
3206—BREAKING THE ICE
3243—AFTER THE ROSES

HARLEQUIN PRESENTS

1352—THE MUSIC OF LOVE

DANGEROUS COMPANY

Kay Gregory

Harlequin Books

TORONTO • NEW YORK • LONDON
AMSTERDAM • PARIS • SYDNEY • HAMBURG
STOCKHOLM • ATHENS • TOKYO • MILAN
MADRID • WARSAW • BUDAPEST • AUCKLAND

With love to FREDA SMITH

Whose courage inspires,
Whose laughter brightens
And whose friendship matters. A lot.

Original hardcover edition published in 1992
by Mills & Boon Limited

ISBN 0-373-17152-8

Harlequin Romance first edition September 1993

DANGEROUS COMPANY

Printed in U.S.A.

CHAPTER ONE

"OOOH, you do have lovely muscles, darling!" gushed a high-pitched feminine voice that sliced through the thin walls of the motel as if they were made of rice paper. "And nice hands too."

Emily opened a sleep-drugged eye and reached wearily for her watch.

Eleven o'clock. She had only been asleep for half an hour, but judging from the sounds coming from next door that might well be all the rest she would get. She sighed, sat up, and turned on the bedside lamp.

"Oooh!" shrieked the piercing voice again. "Ooh, darling, you're so masterful! Are you going to undress me?"

"I think not," replied a distinctive male drawl that hinted strongly of Boston. "I suggest you get on with it yourself."

"All right, darling. Whatever you say."

Emily's sharp ears detected the zing of a zip being enthusiastically lowered, followed by a startled exclamation from the man and a lot of bass-baritone swearing.

"For heaven's sake, woman, you'd better hit that bed fast." The swearing ended abruptly.

Oh, Lord! groaned Emily. Spare me from a night spent listening to Tarzan practicing his ape-man technique on Jane. Because if they're going to keep that up, I might as well forget about sleep.

For a few seconds there was blessed silence, and she began to relax. Perhaps, after all, the tiresome twosome were going to conduct their amours with decent discretion.

Optimist, she jeered at herself a moment later, as the woman let out an annoying, high-pitched giggle and the man rasped something that sounded suspiciously like "silly bitch." Immediately after that a heavy object thudded against the wall just behind Emily's head.

Wonderful, she thought, wondering if there was any point making retaliatory noises herself, and deciding there wasn't. Just wonderful. I make up my mind to spend the night in Campbell River specifically so that I won't have to get up at the crack of dawn, and it turns out I might just as well have stayed home, got at least half a night's sleep, and driven the whole way in the morning.

She jumped, as the wall shuddered again and the man, who appeared to have a remarkably profane line of seduction, uttered a few more pithy epithets that made Emily want to cover her ears. She was about to get out of bed to turn on the television and, with luck, drown out the sordid sounds on the other side of the wall, when she heard a door crash open. Now a third voice, this one thoroughly outraged, joined the two she had already heard.

"What the hell do you think you're doing with my wife?" bellowed this latest participant in what was beginning to sound like a particularly bad bedroom farce.

"Your wife? Oh, good God!" The first man's voice sounded exasperated, but not even remotely apologetic.

"Yes, my wife, you..."

This time Emily did cover her ears.

When she finally lowered her hands again, very tentatively, she heard the woman sniffing noisily and moaning, and the man she had mentally dubbed "Male

Voice Number One'' saying crisply, ''I'll leave her to you, then. Good luck. You'll need it.''

The door closed with a brisk snap.

Heavens, thought Emily, I don't believe it. That man must be one of the biggest rats in town. He's caught red-handed in the middle of seducing someone else's wife, and he hasn't even got the grace to sound guilty! He's lucky he got out of there with his jaw intact. Then she remembered the woman's besotted admiration of his muscles, and felt even more sympathy for the unfortunate husband who, more than likely, weighed a hundred and twenty pounds fully clothed.

She listened for further sounds of warfare but, to her surprise, all she heard was the husband saying resignedly, ''For crying out loud, Vera, why don't you pack it in and get some sleep?''

His words were followed very shortly by the sound of snoring. Male snoring. It was gentle at first, then rose to a crescendo of snorts and bubbles as the night progressed.

Somewhere around four a.m. Emily finally fell asleep with her teeth clenched, only to dream blissfully of the murder of one giggling seductress, one openmouthed snorer and one Tarzan-type Casanova with muscles.

Her alarm went off at precisely half-past six.

She pushed a hand out from under the covers and slammed it off.

At nine o'clock the couple next door began to make sounds of departure. They weren't talking much this morning, but the click of suitcases snapping shut, and the noise of water running, finally penetrated even Emily's sleep-starved brain.

She struggled to a sitting position and glanced anxiously at the clock. It had stopped, but her watch was still going. Damn. If she didn't get a move on, she would miss, yet again, this expedition she had been attempting to make for two years.

An hour and a half later, after a hasty bran muffin breakfast, she was in her little Toyota speeding much too fast along the rain-soaked highway to Gold River.

If that's what I get for trying to be organized, she thought grumpily, why bother?

As it turned out, she needn't have worried, because she arrived at her destination well ahead of the early afternoon departure of the MV *Uchuck III*. An unusual name for a ship, she thought absently, as her eyes lighted on the converted minesweeper which now ferried freight and passengers up Muchalet Inlet to Nootka, where Captain Cook had been the first white man to set foot on Vancouver Island.

She sighed. It was infuriating that after all this anticipation, she was now in such a bad humor, due mainly to lack of sleep and partly to a natural aversion to mornings, that she was in no mood for historic cruises.

"Even if I do owe it to my students," she muttered under her breath.

Along with less colorful subjects, Emily had been teaching a course in local history to a class of eleven- and twelve-year-olds for the last three years. Four times now she had arranged to visit this site of so much history for herself. But Yvonne, the friend she had made the plans with, kept falling in love and deciding she couldn't possibly leave home without Tom, Dick, or Sebastian. Finally, this year, Emily had given up on Yvonne and decided to book the trip on her own. She had chosen the beginning of July so that she would be free to spend the rest of her holidays reading, dreaming, walking her dog and, of course, visiting her widowed mother in Victoria.

Nowadays, of course, she knew that casual tourists weren't allowed to explore the Indian village which Cook had named Friendly Cove. The land remained the property of the Nookahnulth people, although not many of them lived there now. But Emily didn't mind the restrictions. She could still enjoy the scenery, dream of those adventurers of long ago, and soak up atmosphere.

Damp, drizzly atmosphere, she thought morosely, glaring at the dull, gray sky and the wet dock, which was deserted except for a few crew members loading freight. I *would* pick the one lousy day we've had in weeks.

A large drop landed on her head, and she ran for the protection of the covered area.

A few other passengers had arrived by this time, and all of them were gazing disgustedly out at the rain. Then, as Emily glanced at them, she saw one head after another swivel slowly around to the right. In the end, the only person not swiveling was herself.

She brushed at a strand of dark auburn hair which had fallen on her white windbreaker, stared at the ticket booth, studied her feet—and finally gave in to curiosity. Reluctantly her head turned right with the rest.

Her eyes widened. The focus of all the attention was indeed worth looking at.

Tall. Male. Very male, oozing sexuality right up from his booted feet to the blue black hair waving across his forehead. In between was the sort of carved-rock face that looked as though it ought to belong to an Apache chieftain, and a body that any woman would kill to have in her...

No. She pushed the thought out of her mind. *Not* any woman. Not Emily Rogers, for one. She'd had no inclination for that sort of thing for six years, and she certainly wasn't about to start lusting after the first passably attractive man who'd wandered into her orbit for some time. Not that he *was* wandering, she was obliged to admit. On the contrary, he was standing stock still. A leather jacket was slung across his shoulder, and he was resting casually on one smooth, jeans-clad hip. And a very nice hip it was too, she noted. Passably attractive! Who was she trying to kid? The man was gorgeous. And probably lethal.

Trying not to stare too obviously, Emily studied him from under half-lowered lashes. Mmm—nice. Carelessly brushed hair, curiously exotic dark eyes, an aquiline nose, straight eyebrows and surprisingly high bronzed cheekbones. None of these features made him strictly handsome, but he certainly had an aura about him. Which was why every female on the dock was now trying vainly to assume an expression of casual uninterest while continuing to study...the Chieftain. Emily decided there was no other way to describe him.

She also wondered how anyone could pose like a statue for so long without moving. He seemed totally oblivious to the interest he was attracting and, from the rather inflexible line of his lips, she gathered he was not particularly concerned with his surroundings. In fact he appeared to be waiting for something—or someone.

Just then the call came to board the ship, and Emily was forced to tear her gaze away and follow the crowd.

It was still raining, so she settled herself at a table in the small, enclosed passenger cabin. Most of the other travelers were huddled there too, but there was no sign of the man she had dubbed the Chieftain.

"Nice day, isn't it, dear?" An elderly lady with very dyed blond hair eased herself into the opposite seat.

"Is it?" replied Emily doubtfully. To be sure, there was a break in the clouds now, but it was still damp and unseasonably chilly, and she couldn't believe anyone could possibly regard the day as nice.

Apparently this fellow passenger could.

"Of course it is," she trilled enthusiastically. "Every day's a wonderful day if you look on the bright side. There's no such thing as bad weather."

Help! thought Emily, glancing anxiously at the exit. Surely I'm not fated to spend six hours in the company of a dedicated optimist who, any moment now, is going to tell me that every cloud has a silver lining? Because, after a night like last night, I couldn't stand it.

"Into each life a little sleet must fall," she muttered.

"Nonsense, dear. Every cloud——"

A small boy started to scream that he wanted chocolate, his baby sister started to cry, and Emily stood up with more haste than good manners, and gasped, "So sorry. Excuse me. Must have air..." She stumbled out of the cabin and hurried on to the deck.

The breeze stroked lightly at her face, and she breathed it in with relief. At least the rain had stopped now, and anything was better than being cooped up with half a dozen screaming kids and Optimism Personified for the rest of the trip. She moved over to the rail as the engines hummed into service and the ship began to chug down the Inlet. The breeze was stronger here, blowing her long hair around her shoulders, and she took another deep, relaxing breath as she gazed across to the tall trees that seemed to grow straight up out of the water. There were hills behind the trees, she knew, but only the occasional glimpse of a forested slope rose out of the mist to tantalize her imagination as they sailed past.

"Bracing, isn't it?" murmured a voice just behind her left ear. "I'm glad to see there's at least one person on board who doesn't melt at the first sign of bad weather."

Emily jumped as if she'd been punctured by an extra-sharp pin. It *couldn't* be...

But it was. She'd know that unlikely Bostonian drawl if she heard it—well, if she heard it at the bottom of a mine shaft or coming out of a cloud. She ought to. Because of the owner of that voice, she had been dragged from a deep sleep. After which she had spent an exceedingly disrupted night trying to forget the disturbance he had caused.

"The weather's not bad," she responded without looking round. "It's the company I could manage without."

A large, masculine hand closed around the rail beside her slim one. "Is that so?" said the voice. "And I see you also manage without even the rudiments of good manners. Interesting."

Emily's fingers clenched on the rail. "I don't owe you any courtesy," she snapped.

"I think you do." There was something of a threat in the mild way he drawled the words.

"I don't see why." Emily was fighting an irresistible urge to turn round, but she was damned if she'd give him the satisfaction. He'd already ruined her night's sleep, and now he was showing all the classic symptoms of Tarzan on the prowl for a new Jane—to replace the one who had eluded him last night, she supposed.

"You don't see why you owe me a little common politeness?"

"No, I don't."

"For one thing, because you spent several minutes looking me over on the dock, and now it's my turn to do the same for you," the voice replied, with an easy complacency that made Emily want to slap him.

Then, before she could take in what was happening, two firm hands were on her shoulders, and she was being spun round so quickly that she gasped.

When she saw who it was who was treating her with such casual disregard for her dignity, she gasped again.

As she should have guessed, Tarzan and the Chieftain were one and the same.

"You!" she exploded. "Oh, if only I'd known!"

Two straight dark eyebrows rose in unruffled inquiry. "Known what? And what would you have done if you had?"

"I *wouldn't* have looked you over, as you put it. I'd have looked away." Then, realizing what she had just admitted, she added quickly, "I only happened to glance at you by accident. You're not very easy to ignore. Anyway, it was rude of you to notice."

"It wasn't particularly polite of you to do it," he pointed out. "Not that courtesy appears to be one of your strong points. And I could hardly help noticing, could I?" His lip turned up in a cynical little curl. "I suppose I ought to be flattered, but I'm not sure I like being checked over as if I'm a nice piece of steak you're picking out for dinner."

"I don't eat steak," said Emily.

"I'm relieved to hear it," he replied—and she could have sworn his voice shook. "Now—my turn."

She only just had time to draw breath before he was holding her at arm's length, his fingers pressing her shoulders, as his unusual heavy-lidded eyes completed a slow, sensuous appraisal of her body. He started at her feet, continued up over her yellow pants, paused for a moment in the vicinity of her rounded hips and finally came to rest on her face. His expression didn't change at all, and yet Emily felt as if she'd just been peeled naked. She also felt a warm and surprising feeling invade her body, sending a peculiar numbness through her limbs. It was a sensation she hadn't felt for years.

And he's got a very small cleft in his chin, she noted vaguely.

"Yes," he was saying, in a maddeningly cool voice, "that's what I thought."

"What did you think?" asked Emily. She wasn't at all sure she wanted to hear his answer, but she was afraid that if she didn't ask she might regret it.

"I thought you were a very beautiful young woman, as well as a very rude one. Tell me, what have I done to inspire your undying animosity? As I recall, all I did was pass a rather dull comment on the weather."

"I never discuss the weather," said Emily untruthfully, because it happened to be the first thing that came into her head, and she had no intention of discussing the real reason for her animosity.

"All right, we'll talk about something else." His reply was affable enough, but there was a definite edge of steel behind his words.

"I don't want to talk about something else," she retorted. "At least, not with you."

"I see. Well, that's too bad, isn't it? Sometimes all of us have to do things we don't want to."

Emily's mouth opened and then closed again. She couldn't believe the sheer gall of this man. Oh, he was a gloriously sexy male specimen, there wasn't any doubt about that, but surely he didn't think that entitled him to help himself to any woman who happened to take his fancy. Including other people's wives.

"Mr. . . ." she began.

"Silverstone—Aaron Silverstone. And you are . . .?"

"Emily Rogers," she snapped. "Mr. Silverstone, I don't know why you insist on forcing yourself on me——"

"But I'm not forcing myself on you. Or is that wishful thinking, perhaps?"

"*Mr.* Silverstone——"

"Aaron."

Furiously Emily forced herself to look straight at him, instead of at the V where his white shirt met the bronzed skin just below his neck. And she saw that his dark eyes were gleaming with sheer devilment. "*Mr.* Silverstone," she continued through gritted teeth, "you are without a doubt the most obnoxious man I've ever met, and I'd be obliged if you would leave me alone."

"And you are without a doubt the least courteous woman I've ever met, as well as one of the loveliest, and I haven't the slightest intention of leaving you alone."

Emily felt as if she were trapped between the devil on one hand—and two screaming kids and a militant optimist on the other.

"Why?" she asked desperately. "Why won't you just go away?"

"Because I can never resist a challenge, and because I intend to find out why my harmless remark about the weather was met with the equivalent of a fusillade of ice in the face."

"Oh. Then I'll have to complain to the crew."

"Mmm-hmm. And what will you tell them? That a wicked man dared to mention the rain?"

"I'll tell them you're bothering me."

"But I'm not. I'm just talking to you." He grinned suddenly. "Come on, Ms. Sourpuss, let's bury the hatchet and enjoy the scenery together. See, they're heli-logging over there."

His grin was surprisingly disarming, and just for a moment Emily forgot her disrupted night and let her eyes follow the direction of his pointing finger.

The sun had emerged from behind the clouds again, and on a bare brown slope above the water two men were fastening grapples on to logs. Above them a helicopter hovered.

"What are they doing?" asked Emily, fascinated in spite of herself. "It looks dangerous."

"It can be. If they want to avoid getting hit, they have to get out of the way quite smartly once the chopper takes off with the logs."

"Where is it taking them?" Funny, Aaron Silverstone didn't seem quite as obnoxious now that he was playing the nonthreatening role of tour guide.

"To some point where the logging trucks can collect them. You won't be able to see it from here."

"Oh." Emily digested that. "Are you in the logging business, then?"

He laughed. "No, I'm in the travel business. I specialize in tours for people who like to get off the beaten track. That's why I'm here, checking out the lie of the land. Most travelers from my part of the world have heard of Captain Cook, of course, but it's news to them that Captains Bligh and Vancouver sailed with him on the *Resolution* as well."

"I suppose so," said Emily, feeling a little nonplussed. Somehow this man didn't seem the type to sit behind a desk arranging exotic trips for other people.

But then he wasn't behind a desk at the moment, was he? Maybe that was the answer.

She became aware that he was watching her instead of the heli-logging, and she looked up quickly. A long way up. She was five feet eight herself, but he towered above her.

"Feeling better?" he asked, giving her a smile that would have melted her bones if she'd been in any mood to be melted.

"I wasn't ill," she replied, clinging to the memory of last night, but hard-pressed not to respond to his casually seductive charm.

"No. You were just bloody bad-tempered."

"You'd be bad-tempered too if you'd spent the night..." She stopped.

"Yes?" His eyes met hers, and they weren't only gleaming now, they were positively glittering with innuendo. "If I'd spent the night...?"

How she would have got out of that one Emily never knew, because just as she moistened her lips and started to mumble, "Umm—yes, as a matter of fact..." a youthful laugh rang out behind her, followed by the sound of thudding feet, and a second later something alive and rather solid cannoned into her back, shoved her forward, and plastered her up against the rail.

"Tommy!" roared the voice of the man beside her, as she struggled to regain her wind. "For heaven's sake watch where you're going! Emily, are you all right?"

"Yes, yes, I'm all right," she gasped. "Don't worry about it."

"Tommy, apologize at once," snapped Aaron, no longer sounding like a predatory Tarzan who stole other people's wives, but like an ordinary irate parent. "I've told you before, you're not to behave like a damned hooligan!"

"It's all right," repeated Emily, swinging around to face her accidental assailant. "I'm not..." She stopped abruptly.

The child looking up at her with resentful brown eyes had soft, silver beige hair, a small mouth above a prominent chin and a stocky, solid little figure that would probably have been an asset to a rugby team.

The only trouble was that Tommy didn't happen to be a boy. She was a sturdy, rather unattractive little girl whose resentful gaze had now become positively hostile. And obviously this was the someone that Aaron had been waiting for on the dock. His child, and not, as she had half suspected, a woman.

"I'm sorry," Tommy said, in a surly, unapologetic voice. When Emily didn't answer at once, she added woodenly, "You're staring at me like that because I'm ugly, aren't you? Everyone does."

CHAPTER TWO

"TOMMY, for Pete's sake..." Aaron's exasperated voice roused Emily from a paralyzed consternation.

"It's okay," she said quickly, turning at once to Tommy. "I'm sorry, I didn't mean to stare, and of *course* it had nothing to do with your looks. I expected you to be a boy, that's all. Girls aren't usually called Tommy."

"Oh." The hostile gaze wavered for a moment, then fastened on Emily with suspicion. "My name's really Thomasina," she volunteered defiantly.

Emily nodded. "Yes, of course." Privately, she wondered what kind of parent would inflict a name like Thomasina on a child. She glared accusingly at Aaron.

"But you still think I'm ugly, don't you?" Tommy persisted.

"Tommy!" Paternal exasperation was apparently gearing up to full-scale explosion, and suddenly Emily felt sorry for this awkward, unprepossessing little girl.

She directed another glare at Aaron and said firmly, "No, I don't. You've got beautiful hair and lovely skin, and, anyway, ugliness comes much more from inside a person than from their looks. I'll bet you've got a wonderful smile when you use it. Besides, when you're a little older you're sure to look quite different. At least you will if you stop scowling at people."

Tommy's scowl became nothing short of ferocious. "Are you going to tell me the story of the Ugly Ducking?" she demanded.

"Well, I——"

"I thought so." The scowl vanished on a crow of triumph. "Dad's girlfriends always do."

A large hand landed on Tommy's shoulder, and a barely controlled male voice growled furiously, "Tommy, that's quite enough. Emily is not my girlfriend. What the devil's the matter with you, anyway? She's only trying to be kind."

Tommy scuffed a toe along the deck. "I know, but she's beautiful," she said sulkily. "And now you're going to spend the rest of the day trying to kiss her, and you won't have any time left over for me."

"Fat chance," scoffed Aaron. "I defy any man to extract a kiss from Ms. Pins and Needles here. And I always have time for you, you know that."

Tommy comes by it naturally, thought Emily, raising her eyes to the clouds. Rudeness must be a family characteristic. Fleetingly, she wondered what the mother was like, then remembered that Tommy had mentioned girlfriends. Presumably there wasn't a mother. Although with a man like Aaron Silverstone you never knew. After what she had heard last night, she wouldn't put anything past him.

"I'd better be going in," she said abruptly. Even the Optimist and the screaming kids would be better than spending another second in the company of the two Silverstones.

"Don't do that," said Aaron, regaining his equilibrium with apparent ease. "I understand we'll be making a delivery to the camp at Houston River in a minute. You'll want to watch them unloading."

"Will I?" said Emily coldly. "I don't think so."

"You might as well," said Tommy, giving her a small, rather sheepish smile which, as Emily had suspected, improved her appearance considerably. "Once Dad's made up his mind you're going to do something, you have to do it."

Was this an olive branch? Emily decided to take it at face value, and smiled back. "I expect you do if you're his daughter," she agreed. "But you see, I'm not."

Aaron's head turned slowly, and once again his eyes met hers with lazy innuendo. "For which small mercy, I may one day be truly thankful," he murmured, leaving her in no doubt as to the direction of his thoughts.

She tightened her lips. "I'm going in," she snapped.

"Don't be an idiot." He took her elbow. "Everyone else is coming out now, in case you hadn't noticed, so you needn't worry about being without a bodyguard if I should make up my mind to attack you."

He was right. The other passengers were now streaming out onto the deck as the sun made a determined effort to chase away the clouds. And the *Uchuck* was definitely slowing down.

"You won't get the chance to attack me," said Emily haughtily. "And that's no way to speak in front of a child."

"But I'm not in front of a child. Tommy's over there supervising the unloading."

It was true. Tommy, her earlier ill-humor forgotten with amazing ease, was hanging over the rail between a boy her own size and a large lady, watching the busy crew unload barrels of fuel oil, crates of food, and various lumpy packages whose contents would probably remain a mystery.

"I suppose," said Aaron, leading her to an unoccupied corner of the deck, "that you think I should have given Tommy a well-placed smack. In a way I suppose she deserves it."

"I don't think anything of the sort," said Emily hotly. "Her behavior is no worse than yours, and you can see she's unhappy. How on earth could you let her self-image sink so low?"

"I didn't." His voice was clipped. "If you must know, her self-image isn't nearly as bad as she makes out. It just so happens that she's been visiting her mother's parents—who give her everything she wants the moment she wants it. I don't, which always seems to surprise her. Until she gets used to me again." He ran a distracted hand through his already windblown hair. "Unfortunately, this time the situation has been exacerbated by the fact that my daughter happened to overhear her grandmother remarking that she isn't as beautiful as her mother was."

Was? thought Emily. Well, that answered one question. Tommy's mother was dead. She made an effort to mumble sympathetic banalities, and finally came up with, "Oh, dear."

"Quite," agreed Aaron. "And needless to say, Tommy's been milking that one for all it's worth, playing on everyone's desire to spare her feelings—which in fact are remarkably resilient. Sometimes," he added grimly, "I lose patience."

Emily saw that his face looked more like carved rock than ever. And in a way, she sympathized. It couldn't be easy bringing up that active, precocious little girl. But she was surprised at her own feeling of relief that, after all, there didn't appear to be anything seriously wrong with Tommy's emotional well-being. Considering she wouldn't see the child again after today, it really needn't concern her.

"You're a single parent, then?" she said to Aaron now, not wanting him to think she gave a damn, but unable to quell her curiosity.

"Yes—for my sins."

And I'll bet there are plenty of those, thought Emily sourly, once again remembering last night. Poor little Tommy, no wonder she resents it when she sees her father talking to strange women, especially at a time when she hopes to have all his attention for herself. And especially when she's feeling a bit vulnerable about her looks anyway, and the woman her father's talking to happens to be attractive—which she knows she isn't.

Emily was not in the least vain, and she never made any attempt to accentuate her good looks, but after twenty-eight years on the planet, she couldn't help knowing that her long auburn hair, slanting green eyes, straight nose and generous mouth added up to the sort of package that invariably made men look twice. Not that she wanted their attention, she mused glumly. She hadn't wanted any man's attention since David, and the few dates well-meaning friends had arranged for her had been notable only in that neither party had been anxious to repeat the experience. Her fault, of course. She knew that, but somehow she couldn't seem to care.

Vaguely now, she wondered what had happened to Aaron's wife, but after one look at his face, which had gone curiously tight-lipped and distant, she decided it wouldn't be advisable to ask.

The *Uchuck* was proceeding on its course now, and a small coast-guard cutter was moving past them on its way to service the beacons along the Inlet. Tommy ran back toward them.

"I'm going on the upper deck with Jimmy," she informed her father, indicating the boy who had stood beside her at the rail. Then she kicked one foot against the other, shuffled, and mumbled into her chest, "I'm sorry I was rude, Miss..." She hesitated.

"Emily."

"I'm sorry I was rude, Emily, I don't know why I was, and it was nice of you to say you liked my hair."

"I wasn't just saying it," said Emily gently. "It really is very pretty."

Tommy stared at her. "You mean it, don't you?" she said, sounding surprised.

"Of course I do."

Tommy nodded again. "Thank you," she said solemnly. "Come on, Jimmy."

Emily smiled as the two small figures disappeared noisily up the steps.

"Yes. Thank you. And congratulations," said Aaron. "It's not easy to get on Tommy's good side at times like these."

"I can see that," replied Emily shortly.

Thoughtfully he lifted a lock of her long hair and wound it around his finger. "How come a lady who's so short on patience when it comes to a discussion of the weather has all the patience in the world when it comes to my deplorable daughter?"

"She's not deplorable. She probably needs a mother. And I ought to be used to kids, I've been teaching them for seven years. How old is she?

"Eleven. I suppose you wouldn't like to volunteer?"

"Volunteer for what?"

"The position of mother to my brat."

"Don't be ridiculous," said Emily crossly, turning away from the glittering provocation in his eyes.

"I'm not being ridiculous. I think you'd fill the vacancy quite well—once I'd cured you of one or two bad habits."

Emily shook her head disbelievingly. Over the years, she'd been the object of every seduction technique in the book, not to mention some that hadn't been thought of. But this man absolutely took the cake. He was versatile too, she reflected wryly, once again remembering last night. The ape-man technique had been working splendidly on Vera until he had been so summarily interrupted.

"You're not curing me of anything, Mr. Silverstone," she said flatly. "And I don't want to be anybody's mother."

"The name's Aaron. And if motherhood doesn't appeal to you, how about the idea of being someone's wife? They could go together, you know."

No. She just didn't believe this. She'd known the man less than half a day, and already he was *proposing* to her. Or was he? She glanced at his face and saw the silver lights glinting in his eyes. No, he wasn't proposing. He was baiting her. Very successfully too, she had to admit. All the same, she'd had about enough of it. And of him.

"Mr. Silverstone," she said firmly, "you've had your fun, and this time I *am* going in."

The lock of hair was still held loosely in his fingers, and she jerked it away. But instead of trying to prevent her escape he merely smiled—a slow, curving smile that made her heart slam hard against her ribs. It was an unexpected sensation. One she hadn't felt for—too long.

No. No, she didn't mean that. It was a sensation she had no desire to feel again. No desire whatsoever.

Without looking at him now, she turned on her heel and bolted like a rabbit for the door.

The sun disappeared again the moment Emily settled herself in her seat. But the children had stopped screaming at last, and the Optimist was now pouring her brand of good cheer over a cowed and captive audience from Toronto, she was content to watch the quiet gray slopes drift past from the comfortable security of the cabin.

The *Uchuck* stopped at a fishing camp and then at several logging camps, while Emily remained below, observing the activity on the docks with interest, and trying to keep her mind focused on the scenery. But all the time, as she saw oil drums and crates being lowered over the side, and heard the crew and the local residents bandy greetings, she was conscious that Aaron Silverstone was out there somewhere. She was determined not to encounter him again.

At last, as they rounded Bligh Island near the mouth of the Sound, someone announced over a loudspeaker that they were approaching their destination. At that point Emily knew she couldn't hide any longer if she intended to fulfill her purpose in making this trip. Reluctantly, she sidled out onto the deck to press herself unobtrusively against a bulkhead.

"Decided to risk it, did you?" murmured a mocking voice in her ear.

"Risk what?" She sighed, making no effort to disguise the fact that she didn't appreciate the intrusion.

"My dangerous company, of course."

"Believe it or not, I wasn't even thinking about you," lied Emily. "I came out to get a good view of Friendly Cove and Nootka."

"Mmm. Well, you're getting one." Aaron raised a long arm and pointed across green, surging water to the headland where a red-roofed lighthouse, a small church, and one or two single-story houses stood in picturesque isolation against the sky. The sun, making yet another attempt to defeat the grayness, came out again at that moment to touch the roofs with a pale, translucent gold. Behind them the blue green hills of Nootka rose gently beneath pearl-tinted clouds.

"It looks lonely but rather lovely, doesn't it?" said Emily, as the ship stopped at the end of a long wooden dock that protruded out into the water. "I can see why those old-time sailors called it Friendly."

"Aha. Do I detect the beginnings of a thaw?" inquired Aaron, placing an arm casually over her shoulder as the crew began to unload the usual supplies, along with a consignment of household furniture which a cheerful trio of locals were hurrying out to pick up.

"Thaw? What thaw?" Emily tried to wriggle away, but he wouldn't let her. She was still attempting to decide whether to shout for help or kick him, when she saw the family on the dock wave goodbye, and a few seconds later the engine started up yet again. A short while after that the *Uchuck* steamed around the point and out into the open Pacific. Here the swell of the ocean was unexpectedly strong. Emily stumbled and almost lost her balance as the ship's loudspeaker suddenly blared the information that the cairns dedicated to the memory of Captain Cook and Vancouver were now in view. The noise made her jump, so that if Aaron hadn't tightened his grip she would have fallen against the rail.

"I meant a thaw in your attitude," he said lightly. "For a moment there I thought you might actually be about to forgive me for daring to bring up the subject of the weather."

"Oh, do stop going on about the weather!" she snapped. "And no, you don't detect a thaw."

She did, though. The feel of his firm body alongside hers, and the pressure of his hand on her arm through the flimsy fabric of her windbreaker, were sending all kinds of hot messages through her veins. And if that wasn't a thaw, she didn't know what was. But all the same, it had to stop.

The instant the ship returned to the more sheltered waters of the Sound, she looked up at him and said in the iciest voice she could muster, "Please take your hands off me, Mr. Silverstone."

"Hand," he corrected her. "Just one of them."

"All right, *hand*," she conceded through clenched teeth. "Please take it off me."

"With pleasure," he replied, stepping back with unflattering alacrity. "I'll go and warm it up on an iceberg."

"You do that," agreed Emily, annoyed by the iceberg allusion. Contrarily, now that he was no longer touching her, she realized she had liked the feel of his tough body standing next to hers. She liked the look of the back of him as well.

He had turned away from her now and was staring down at the water, with one booted foot resting on the rail and the wind blowing his white shirt about him like a sail. Slowly her eyes dropped down, and she was half guiltily admiring the way the tight denim stretched across his much-too-alluring male backside, when he swung around.

She didn't quite have time to wipe the look of glazed approval off her face.

"Well, well, well," murmured Aaron, his eyes all caressing black velvet. "Maybe I needn't look for that iceberg after all. By the way, you're welcome to touch the merchandise if you like."

"Oh, you—you're impossible!" Furious with herself, and furious that she hadn't been able to hide a blush, Emily spun around and went into her rabbit-on-the-run act for the second time that afternoon.

But just before the door shut behind her a soft chuckle rose above the sound of the engine, and a very sexy male voice purred silkily, "I assure you, I'm very possible, darling. Why don't you try me and see?"

Emily muttered a few choice words her mother would not have approved, and for the remainder of the journey back to Gold River she sat with her head in her hands, hoping the people around her would take her for a victim of migraine. Not that she'd ever had a migraine, but at the moment that didn't seem to matter. The only thing that did matter was that Aaron Silverstone should be dissuaded from coming near her again.

She didn't see him after that until the ship docked, and she was just diving for her car and congratulating herself on the success of her evasive tactics when she felt a hand on her elbow, and that voice she'd hoped she wouldn't hear again said, "What's the hurry, darling? Tommy and I were hoping you'd have dinner with us tonight."

"I'm not your darling, and I can't," said Emily, sliding swiftly behind the wheel. "I have to be back in Cinnamon Bay this evening."

"Do you now? So where and what is Cinnamon Bay?"

"It's where I live. A seaside town about halfway between here and Victoria."

"In that case you'll need to eat first."

"No, I won't. I had a sandwich on the boat. I'm not hungry."

"I think you are." Aaron rested a hand on the roof of the Toyota and bent down so that his face was almost touching hers. "I think you're very hungry indeed."

Startled, Emily stared into eyes that were holding her in the sort of gaze she imagined the Inquisition had once reserved for its more recalcitrant customers. It wasn't the sort of gaze one lied to, either. And she knew he wasn't talking about food.

"No," she croaked, lying anyway. "No, you're wrong. I'm—not hungry. Not—not at all."

"Liar," he said softly.

She'd known it wouldn't do any good. "I'm not lying," she began hopelessly.

"Yes, you are. But have it your own way. Gold River is a charming little town, but if you won't stay to eat with us perhaps Tommy and I will press on to Campbell River."

Emily frowned. He wasn't even going to make an effort to change her mind, then—a fact which didn't please her as much as she'd expected. And now she wouldn't dare stop in Campbell River either for fear of running into him again. That meant she'd be starving by the time she finally got home.

"Yes, why don't you do that?" she muttered, not looking at him. "Bye, Tommy. Take care. I enjoyed meeting you." She waved to the little girl who was hovering doubtfully in the background, and started up the engine of her car.

In a moment Aaron and Tommy were nothing more than two black specks behind her on the road.

It wasn't until she was well past Campbell River that she felt it was safe to relax in the certainty that by this time Aaron and Tommy would be filling their faces in some elegant restaurant—with a substantial menu—that possibly even served chocolate cake with ice cream...

Emily licked her lips and mentally cursed Aaron Silverstone for about the hundredth time that day.

"Emily Rogers, you're a fool. You could have accepted his invitation," whispered a traitorous little voice inside her head.

"Oh, no, I couldn't," she answered it. "Life's already knocked me into one hole that I've had a hell of a time crawling out of. The last thing I need now is to get myself involved, even temporarily, with a man who thinks he owns the world as well as anybody's wife he fancies. Even if he is the most mouth-watering hunk I've met since..."

She got no farther. Just as she rounded a sharp bend, the car lurched crazily, and she felt a strong pull to the right.

"Oh, no!" she groaned, rolling her eyes to the heavens. "No. Please, not now. Honestly, I couldn't stand it!"

But whoever she was praying to wasn't listening.

She bumped and jerked her way to the side of the highway, climbed out and, with her heart in her mouth, bent down to inspect the damage. Just as she had feared, it was as plain as the large spot of grease on her yellow pants that her right front tire had recently lost an argument with a nail.

Glumly she stared down at the offending wheel. At least it wasn't dark yet and, theoretically, she did know how to change a tire.

But a few minutes later she was forced to admit that theory had very little connection with hard fact.

"Damn you, David," she muttered. "You and your stupid powder-puff mechanics! What the hell was the use of *showing* me, if you weren't going to actually let me do it?"

She picked up a wrench, but it didn't do much good, because she still had very little idea what to do with it.

"And it wasn't fair of you to die on me either," she said, giving the collapsed tire a vicious kick.

That didn't help either, and determinedly she made herself think back to the day when David had insisted that she learn how to do minor repairs. Perhaps if she concentrated, she would remember...

She scowled down at the ground and concentrated on concentrating. But in the end all she remembered was that David's idea of teaching had involved doing the job himself while she watched. The result, she was obliged to acknowledge gloomily as she threw the wrench back into the trunk, was that although she now had the spare out and ready to put on, and the jack tilted at an unlikely angle under the car, this was about as far as she was going to get.

Sighing, she gazed hopefully at the road. A long stream of cars hurtled past, but as the sun was already sinking into the sea across the highway, everyone was in a rush to get home.

Hesitantly she moved closer to the traffic and raised her hand. No one stopped. Then, just as she was beginning to think she had better start looking for a phone, someone did stop.

And Emily wished he hadn't.

The man striding toward her from a beat-up old pickup wore a black leather jacket, a dirty T-shirt, ill-fitting jeans and a leer. He also sported an unkempt beard and tattoos on the backs of both hands.

"Trouble, sweetheart?" he inquired, as his eyes roamed over her with something that looked horribly like anticipation.

"Yes, but..." Emily hesitated, wondering if it would be wise to point out that she wasn't his sweetheart.

The leer became more pronounced. "Thought so. What'll you give me if I fix it for you, then?"

"Well, I'm willing to pay..."

"Sure you are. In advance." He wasn't leering any more, he was moving toward her with a rolling, powerful gait, and two hamlike hands were reaching for her waist.

Emily stepped back. "What are you doing? I meant I'll pay you money." She glanced frantically at the road, but now, when her need was desperate, inevitably there wasn't a car in sight. Only an empty ribbon of highway winding its way along the coast, and bounded on this side by trees.

"I don't want money, sweetheart. I want you."

"But you can't—someone'll see you..." She tried to squirm away from him as he dug his hands into her shoulders, then slid them down to grab her around the waist.

Her attempt at escape had come too late. And anyway, she thought frantically, it would have been a losing battle, because he really was a very big man—who stank quite overpoweringly of beer.

Oh, God, this couldn't be happening. It was still daylight, and they were at the side of a busy highway. Surely this had to be a nightmare. She must have fallen asleep at the wheel...

But as his slack mouth approached her face, and his foul breath almost knocked her over, she knew with appalled horror that what was about to happen was going to be a whole lot worse than any nightmare. If she didn't do something.

Summoning every reserve of strength she had ever possessed, she lifted her knee and aimed it where it would do the greatest damage. But she was off balance, and she missed her target.

The man swore. "I'll get you for that!" he grunted.

"Like hell you will!" Suddenly Emily was too angry to be frightened. Who did this ape think he was?

She lifted her knee again, but this time her attacker sidestepped, caught the upraised limb, and tipped her backward. Hard ground slammed against her back, and she could feel gravel scrape along her palms as, automatically, she held them out to cushion the fall.

Then, as she closed her eyes against the pain, she was conscious that his heavy body was half on top of her, his hands fumbling at the zip of her windbreaker. She braced herself for one superhuman effort to throw him off, at the same time twisting her head away so his mouth couldn't reach her lips. And in that moment, to her utter disbelief and relief, his fingers loosened.

Emily blinked, taking in that a large bronzed hand had seized her assailant by the shoulder, swung him around, and landed a neat and crunchingly efficient punch on his bearded jaw.

It didn't knock him out, but the impact made him stagger, and after one look into the blazing black eyes of her rescuer, Emily's attacker turned on his heel and stumbled drunkenly in the direction of his pickup.

"Thank you," she whispered hoarsely, accepting the hand outstretched to help her. "Thank you so much..." She pressed her knuckles against her eyes, starting to shiver now that the ordeal was over. Once again she wondered if she was dreaming. It couldn't be...

But it was.

Aaron Silverstone, with both hands on his hips, was glaring down at her, not with concern or sympathy, but in exactly the same way he'd glared at Tommy back at the boat.

"Have you lost your mind?" he demanded harshly. "Don't you have enough sense to stay in your car, instead of cavorting around the highway in a pair of pants that look like an open invitation to a good time?"

Emily gasped. "They—they don't look like——" She broke off as Aaron caught her wrist, pushed it behind her back and pressed her hand over the area that the pants were supposed to cover.

She wanted desperately to hit him. The only trouble was, he was right. The pants didn't cover much at all. The center seam appeared to have split from top to bottom. Open they certainly were, no doubt displaying an intriguing view of her white lace bikini panties.

"Oh!" she groaned. "I thought I felt something go when I was trying to change my tire. But I didn't pay much attention..."

She shook her head dazedly. No wonder that horrible drunk had stopped! And no wonder Aaron thought...

"All right," she said, taking a long gulping breath, and keeping her hand, which still stung a bit, firmly clasped over the rip, "so I had an accident. But it's not my fault, and I had to get out of the car because I had a flat. How was I to know that big lout...?" She stopped, as the beat-up pickup suddenly roared to life and sped off hell for leather down the highway. "He's drunk," she said. "We have to stop him."

"No," said Aaron. "The police do. This isn't Gotham City, and I've no intention of playing Batman to your

Vicki What's-Her-Name. Come on, get in my car and we'll stop at the nearest phone."

"But what about——?"

"Don't worry, I'll drive you back."

Emily nodded, too exhausted now to argue. And anyway, he was right as usual. Her drunken assailant mustn't be allowed to create further havoc along the highway.

Aaron's car, somewhat to her surprise, turned out to be a rather ordinary gray station wagon with "Silverstone Travel" emblazoned in bright silver letters along the side. Tommy, breathing softly, was fast asleep in the back.

An hour and a half later, after a brief visit to the closest police station, they were on their way back to pick up Emily's car.

"I'm sorry," said Aaron abruptly.

"Sorry? What for?" Emily was still too shattered to think straight.

"For chewing your head off about your pants when you'd just had what must have been a very frightening experience."

"Oh," said Emily, "that." At this stage she had more to worry about than Aaron's moods. "It doesn't matter. Why did you?"

"Why did I what?"

"Chew my head off?"

"I suppose because the sight of you being mauled about by that drunken lout made me lose my temper. And landing one punch on his jaw wasn't quite enough to work it off."

"I see. So you worked it off on me instead."

"That's about the size of it."

"You don't *sound* very sorry."

"You mean I'm not groveling sufficiently?" She saw one eyebrow slant up in artless inquiry, heard the quiver of amusement in his voice, and gave up.

"You don't, do you?" she said resignedly. "Grovel, I mean."

"Nope."

"Oh, well, never mind." She shrugged. "I suppose I'll have to let it pass. After all, you did rescue me. *And* you loaned me a blanket so I'd be decent." She touched the red tartan blanket that was now wrapped securely around her waist.

"I did, didn't I? Misguided of me. Indecency suited you much better."

Emily took one look at the provocative light in his eye and made up her mind to ignore it. "That reminds me," she said—it didn't, but it seemed a good thing to say "—what were you doing following so close behind me? I thought you were going to eat in Campbell River."

"We did. Hamburgers."

Emily shuddered. "That explains it. I was sure you were guzzling a gourmet meal—complete with chocolate cake and ice cream."

Aaron heard the wistful note in her voice, and grinned. "I thought you said you weren't hungry," he said innocently.

"Oh, shut up!" Emily's nerves were already on edge, and she wasn't in any mood for his banter.

"Keep up that tone with me, young lady, and I'll dump you on the side of the road and let you fix your own flat tire."

"No, you won't," said Emily with certainty. "You're not like that."

"Maybe not, but I'm very capable of making you do the work yourself. It might do you good."

"Actually it would. I should be able to fix it myself."

"Mmm," said Aaron, "you should." He spun the wheel expertly to the left and brought the station wagon to a stop beside her Toyota. "And if it wasn't so late, and if you were up to it, I'd see to it that you learned. As it is, provided you keep a curb on that tongue of yours, we'll postpone the lesson until later."

Emily was too weary now to point out that there wasn't going to be a later, and as she was also too weary to make the effort herself, she stood quietly holding the flashlight for Aaron while he removed the useless wheel and attached her spare. It was dark now, but he hadn't put on a jacket, and as Emily stood staring down at him, she couldn't help admiring the strength and breadth of his shoulders, and the play of muscles in his forearms where he had pushed the loose white sleeves of his shirt above his elbows.

Had it really been almost six years...?

Aaron worked with practiced efficiency, and in a very short space of time the spare was in place.

"Right," he said, wiping his hands on a rag, "that's that. Now, do you suppose you can make it home without collapsing?"

"Of course." Emily was very much on her dignity.

"Good. Then I suggest you drive on ahead. I'll follow behind to make sure you don't run into any more trouble."

"Oh, there's no need for that," she said quickly. "I'll be fine."

"I wouldn't count on it. Don't you know your spare is practically bald?"

"Is it?" she said vaguely. "Yes, I guess the garage did say something——"

"Which you chose to ignore, I suppose." Aaron's tone was severe. "It figures."

"It doesn't figure," retorted Emily, irritated. "I just didn't think of it."

"Precisely. So now the only thing that makes any sense is for you to get off your high horse and into your car, because, whether you like it or not, I intend to follow you home. After spending half my evening sorting you out, I might as well finish the job."

"Sorting—finish the... But you weren't even going to Cinnamon Bay," protested Emily.

"How do you know?"

"I don't, but——"

"As a matter of fact I wasn't going anywhere in particular. I'm just exploring Vancouver Island. One stop is as good as another."

"Stop?" Emily heard the squeak in her voice, and made a hasty effort to lower it to a normal level. "What do you mean, stop?"

Aaron directed the flashlight pointedly at his watch. "In case you haven't noticed, it's getting late, and I have a sleeping child in my car. I'm prepared to escort you home, but I'm not planning on traveling any farther."

"But you can't stay with me," objected Emily. "You've been very helpful, and I *am* grateful, but——"

"But you're not about to spend the night with the Big Bad Wolf," he interrupted dryly. "I suppose that means you live alone. However, as a night of passion wasn't actually what I had in mind, I imagine there *are* hotels in Cinnamon Bay?"

Did he *have* to sound so superior? Night of passion indeed! He *was* a dreamer. "One," she said briefly. "The

Inn on the Beach. And three motels. But they might be full."

"Shall we cross that bridge when we come to it? And can we please stop wasting time and get this cavalcade on the road?

Emily glared at him, then realized there wasn't much point in it because in this light he couldn't see her expression. Lifting her chin, she opened the door of the Toyota and got in. "I'll stop at the Inn," she said briskly. "They're the best bet. I can make my own way home from there."

"Afraid to let me know where you live?" he asked caustically.

"Of course not. I just want to make sure you find a bed."

As she switched on the engine, she thought she heard his laconic voice drawl, "How encouraging!"

She slammed the door extra hard.

The station wagon followed her closely all the way down the curving highway. Once or twice, out of sheer contrariness, Emily tried to elude it. Then she remembered that she wasn't innately hard to get along with and that Aaron had been extraordinarily kind. Why almost everything he said had the effect of turning her into someone she normally wasn't, she didn't know. All she did know was that she didn't like it.

When they finally reached the outskirts of Cinnamon Bay she saw that, as she had half expected, the first two motels they passed were full. So was the third one a few miles farther down the bay. Which left the Inn, but in spite of what she had told Aaron she didn't think that would be a problem.

In that she turned out to be wrong. The Inn, to the delight of the management, and the disgruntlement of the harried staff, was bursting at the seams with librarians.

"But don't you have *anything*?" pleaded Emily, as she hovered beside Aaron in Reception and tried to look as though she always dressed in blankets.

"Afraid not, Em." Annie Stokes, behind the desk, shook her head. "Our librarians are holding their convention here, you see."

"Never mind," said Aaron. "I'm sure we'll think of something."

As they walked toward the exit, Emily was certain that Annie's birdlike gaze was riveted with deep suspicion on their backs. She was also certain that Annie had jumped to her own conclusions as to the sort of something they would think of.

She was still casting frantically about for a polite way to tell Aaron he'd have to look for accommodation down the highway, when they reached the parking lot, and saw that Tommy had woken up at last. She was sitting on the edge of her seat dazedly rubbing at her eyes.

"Can we stop now, Dad?" she asked, looking very young and pathetic. "Please, I want to go to bed."

CHAPTER THREE

AARON cast an enigmatic glance at Emily. "How far's the nearest town?" he asked, in a voice that managed to sound detached and coolly accusing at the same time.

"About fifteen miles. Unless you have a tent—there's a campground just down the road."

"Tommy can't tent. She has allergies."

"Mmm, my skin breaks out and I sneeze," mumbled Tommy sleepily. "Then I'm even uglier." She lifted a heavy eyelid and searched Emily's face for a reaction.

"Couldn't resist it, could you?" said Aaron caustically. "Even when you're only half awake."

Tommy's solid little face crumpled, and she looked almost ready to burst into tears. "Dad, can't we stay here?" she pleaded.

"They don't have room for us."

Emily knew when she'd been backed into a corner. Tommy might be laying it on with a trowel, as Aaron had hinted, but she *was* sleepy. And she certainly wasn't very pretty. It was impossible not to feel sorry for the child.

"My cottage is just up the hill," she said to Aaron, not troubling to put any enthusiasm into the offer. "It only has one bedroom, but I can put a cot in there for Tommy, if you like, and there's a sofa bed in the living room for you."

"Your hospitality overwhelms me," said Aaron, who hadn't failed to notice her reluctance. "However, for the sake of my daughter, I'm afraid I'll have to accept."

"I thought you would." Emily still couldn't hide her resentment that, because of an unlikely series of events, she was beholden to this man who last night had ruined her sleep while attempting to seduce someone called Vera. And if that was anything to go by, no doubt he'd try to ruin tonight for her as well.

But her name wasn't Vera.

"Don't worry," he said, interrupting her thoughts with devastating perception, "Tommy makes an excellent chaperone."

Oh, yeah, thought Emily. In that case, where was Tommy last night? But she didn't ask the question out loud. Instead she tossed her head and told him to follow her up the hill.

A few minutes later the Toyota was bumping its way down the unpaved lane that ended abruptly in front of her home. Sighing irritably, she jerked to a stop, flung open the door and jumped out in front of a rustic cedar shake cottage that was nestled unexpectedly in a clearing beneath a grove of fir trees. Aaron's car pulled up right behind her.

"Nice place," he said, lifting a semiconscious Tommy out of his car and holding her as if she were no weight at all. "It's exactly the sort of place I thought you'd have."

"Why?" asked Emily warily.

"Secluded, out of the way. Somewhere you can avoid unnecessary contact with the world."

"I'm not exactly a hermit," she replied, annoyed. "I have a neighbor down the lane, several friends in town and a teaching job that keeps me pretty busy."

"And a peephole when you want to hide from them all," said Aaron, sticking to his original assessment.

Emily frowned and didn't answer as she turned away from his massive form outlined against the moonlight. He looked like some primeval god standing there with his legs apart and holding the sleeping child in his arms. But, godlike or not, he was irritating her almost beyond belief. Partly, she was forced to admit, because he was right about her need for a peephole...

It hadn't always been like that, though. Six years ago she'd been surrounded by people, with a challenging job, a busy home life—and David.

"Why?" she whispered for the thousandth time, as her mind moved back down the years. "Why, David?" She wasn't even conscious that in the stillness of the night her soft, unhappy murmur hung audibly in the air above the clearing.

Closing her eyes against the pain that never stayed away for long, she jabbed her key into the lock as if it were a dagger that could expunge all feeling from her heart.

Behind her, Aaron's eyes narrowed, but he said nothing as he kicked the door and followed her into a blue-walled bedroom where she was already pulling a fold-up bed out of a closet.

"I'll do that," he said, his eyebrows lifting slightly as he laid Tommy on the queen-size brass bed. Then he took his hostess firmly by the shoulders and moved her out of the way.

Emily, who hadn't missed the angle of his eyebrows, started self-consciously when he touched her and hurried out to the kitchen muttering under her breath about coffee.

The eyebrows rose even further and were complemented by a long, very speculative smile.

The smile was still there when, after settling Tommy on the extra bed, Aaron strolled out to the kitchen just in time to catch a promising view of Emily's white lace bikini panties as she unfastened the blanket and tried to hitch it more securely about her waist.

"Who's the lucky man?" he inquired lazily, draping himself around the doorframe.

"What lucky man?" asked Emily, blushing furiously.

"The one who gets the benefit of the panties. Or rather the privilege of taking them off." His engaging grin took most of the offense out of the words, but it didn't help much. She still felt mortified.

"How dare you?" she snapped. "I dress to please myself, not for the benefit of any *man*, and if you think——"

"I wasn't talking about dressing, actually," he interrupted. "Rather the opposite. And I'm not accusing you of murder, my dear. It's hardly a crime to be human."

"Like you, I suppose," she scoffed. "I know all about your kind of humanity."

"Do you now? How very interesting. And what kind of humanity is that?"

Quite suddenly the fight went out of Emily. There was no point in sparring with this impossible man. It only seemed to provoke him to further heights of inexcusable innuendo. Hadn't he said something earlier about enjoying a challenge? He was probably the kind of man who thrived on opposition, and the last thing she wanted was to encourage him.

"It doesn't matter," she said tiredly. "Can we just have something to eat and go to bed?"

"A most stimulating suggestion," he said, grinning. "But I'm not at all sure I'm up to it tonight."

Emily glowered, but the grin only broadened. Oh, he was up to it all right, she fumed silently. There wasn't any doubt about that. But the question at this moment was whether she was up to slapping his face.

Once again Aaron seemed to read her thoughts. "I wouldn't advise it," he said quietly, moving away from the door and pulling out a chair from the white arborite table. "Now, what was that you said about eating?"

So he expected maid service too. Emily was just about to tell him she wasn't a servant, when she remembered that he was only here because he'd stopped to help her out. She supposed she owed him a meal. Hamburgers probably weren't enough for a man his size.

"I'm making alfalfa and tofu sandwiches," she informed him.

"You're making *what*?" If she hadn't been so tired, Emily would have laughed out loud at the expression of outrage on his face.

"Alfalfa and tofu sandwiches," she repeated sweetly.

"Oh. That's what I thought you said." He fixed a dubious eye on a package of oat bran on the counter, and asked plaintively, "Don't you have any *food*?"

"Of course. I told you, tofu and——"

"I meant *edible* food. Ham, or a pork chop or something."

"I don't eat meat, Mr. Silverstone."

He stared at her, then stretched his long legs in front of him and raised his eyes to the ceiling. "Good Lord! You mean it, don't you?" he groaned. "When you told me you didn't eat steak——"

"I meant I didn't eat steak," she agreed coolly.

"And because I do, that makes me a self-indulgent glutton, I suppose."

He looked so disgusted and so pessimistic—presumably about the prospects of a decent meal—that in spite of her weariness Emily couldn't help giggling. Besides, she *had* been intentionally sanctimonious. The opportunity had been too attractive to pass up.

"No, of course it doesn't," she conceded, relenting. "You have a perfect right to eat anything you please—within reason."

"Thank you."

"You're quite welcome."

Aaron fixed her with a skeptical eye. "I don't suppose standing on my rights will do me much good at the moment, though, will it? I appear to have a magnificent choice of tofu, alfalfa or oat bran."

Emily giggled again, and Aaron's set features relaxed a little. Ms. Emily Rogers was a knockout even when she was spitting at him. When she smiled, she had the face of an angel.

"It's not that bad," she answered him. "I do have eggs or cheese if you prefer it."

"I prefer it."

"Fine," said Emily. "Just give me time to change into a respectable pair of pants, and I'll see what I can whip up." She darted out of the kitchen before he could make the inevitable comment about the blanket being more than adequate covering.

When she returned, Aaron was still stretched out in the chair, staring around him with an expression of incredulity.

"How do you ever find anything in all this clutter?" he asked, gesturing at the collection of pots, pans and boxes that littered the counter, along with several piles of magazines, two tennis balls, a broken flower vase and three baking tins loaded with junk mail.

"Easy," said Emily cheerfully. "I never put anything away, and that way everything's always at hand."

Aaron shook his head.

"The cheese is a bit moldy," she added, peering doubtfully into the fridge. "But the bread's okay. How about a fried egg sandwich?"

He nodded, apparently speechless.

A few minutes later the kitchen was filled with the fumes of burning oil, and an egg, blackened around the edges, was being shoveled onto a slice of whole wheat bread.

"I'm afraid it's a bit overcooked," said Emily unnecessarily, as she placed the burnt offering in front of Aaron, and sat down across from him to consume her mashed alfalfa and tofu with obvious and overdramatized relish.

"Mmm," he said, displaying unusual restraint as he successfully swallowed a mouthful without gagging. "What other surprises do you have in store for me, Ms. Rogers?"

"Surprises?"

"In the past half hour I've learned that you sleep in a queen-size bed—that's the encouraging part—that you can successfully navigate your way around a kitchen that hasn't one flat surface visible to the naked eye, that you don't eat meat, and that your cooking——"

"Leaves something to be desired," finished Emily wryly. "I know it does. But I never had much time to learn when I was—well, when I lived in Victoria. And my mother can't bear anyone else in her kitchen. Now that I'm on my own, there doesn't seem much point."

"Of course there's a point," said Aaron. "For heaven's sake, woman, you'll ruin your health if all you live on is rabbit food that you can't even be bothered to cook!"

"It's not rabbit food," objected Emily, ignoring the reference to her lack of culinary enthusiasm. She was also endeavoring to forget that suggestive reference to her big bed.

He sighed. "If you say so. Why *don't* you eat meat, Emily?"

"Because I prefer my furry things on the hoof to on the plate," she replied simply.

"Oh, one of those." Aaron eyed her as if she had told him she belonged to a sorority dedicated to the preservation of muffins, and heaved another long, lugubrious sigh.

"Yes, one of those," she retorted, with a steely note in her voice. "Do you have some problem with that?"

"No, not at all," he said hastily, trying not to think about breakfast. He choked down the last of the egg. "Thank you, Emily. I appreciate the effort."

"But not the results," she said ruefully.

"Well..."

"It's all right, you don't have to be polite. You never are anyway."

"You malign me."

"No, I don't."

He tapped his fingers on the table, studying her with a pensive look. "In that case," he said eventually, "since I can't win with you anyway, I think perhaps now's the time to bring up another, more serious matter that you probably won't want to hear about either."

"What's that?" asked Emily suspiciously.

"That if you continue to drive like the maniac I followed down the highway this evening, you're likely to end up cooling your pretty heels in jail. It's time you had some sense knocked into you, Emily Rogers, before you kill someone."

Emily gaped at him, hurt and indignant. For a while there he had actually been quite human, even when he was telling her how to run her life, because that had seemed motivated more by concern than anything else. But now he was looking at her like a judge considering his verdict, and there was no concern or softness in his words, or about the grim set of his mouth.

All at once she felt horribly tired. She'd had a frightening, exhausting evening, she didn't want this man complicating her life—and she'd had about as much of him as she could take.

"I'm going to bed now," she said, standing up quickly, and turning away from him, so he wouldn't see the tears she was fighting back. "I've put clean sheets in the living room, so all you have to do is pull out the sofa when you're ready."

She ran toward the door, aware that if she stayed in the room with him one second longer she was likely to collapse in a howling heap on the floor.

"Hey, hold it!"

The voice behind her was exasperated, but surprisingly gentle, and she hesitated a fraction too long. Just as she reached the door she felt two firm hands on her shoulders pulling her backward, and then she was trapped against the length of Aaron's body as his arms locked around her rib cage, holding her fast.

"Hey, I'm sorry," he murmured, his lips a few centimeters above her ear. "I didn't realize—you're all in, aren't you? I should have guessed."

It was too much. His censure she could cope with—just. His kindness completely unraveled her.

"I—I'm not—not really a maniac," she sobbed. "I was upset. I kept thinking of that horrible man, and I couldn't concentrate..."

"Of course you couldn't," he agreed soothingly. "I should have had the sense to insist on driving you home. And of course you're not a maniac—at least I hope not. You're just a lousy cook." When her sobs only increased, he added on a note of alarm, "For heaven's sake, Emily, I was kidding!"

Making a determined effort to halt the waterworks, Emily leaned back against him, aware of a surprising sense of security and warmth—as well as of something much more immediate. Aaron moved his hands to her waist, turned her slowly around, and pressed her head against his chest.

They stood that way for several seconds, not moving, then Emily felt his fingers beneath her chin, tilting her face up.

His lips weren't so hard now, but they looked wonderfully firm—and seductive. She couldn't take her eyes off them.

He stared down at her, frowning, and Emily thought she saw a look of surprise cross his face. Then surprise was replaced by resolution. Before she realized what he meant to do, he had bent his head, and those devastating lips were brushing lightly over her forehead. Then over her nose...

She opened her mouth to protest, but he closed it at once with a kiss—a warm and very gentle kiss that awakened in her feelings so long forgotten that for a few brief seconds she thought Aaron was no more than a bittersweet dream.

All urge to protest vanished then on a wave of unexpected and overwhelming sweetness. No longer aware of what she was doing, Emily made a small sound in her throat and lifted her hands to tangle them in his hair. Immediately both his arms swept around her waist, and, although he was holding her loosely, she found that she could hardly breathe. But perhaps she didn't need to breathe, she thought wildly. There wasn't any air in her lungs, and yet she felt alive, exhilarated as she hadn't been in years.

His kiss deepened as he sensed her response, and the lips that had touched hers so softly became harder, more demanding. His hands moved lower, pressing her against him so that she could feel the muscular tautness of his thighs...

Muscular... Oh, Lord! she thought. Somewhere in the back of her mind a door opened and an unwanted memory sidled in. A memory of a woman's voice gurgling about lovely muscles, and a man's voice growling that she'd better hit that bed...

"Oh!" she cried, wrenching her lips away and putting both hands against his chest. "Don't—don't, please, Aaron! Stop!"

He stopped at once.

"What is it?" he asked, eyes narrowing as he put a distance of at least a foot between them. "What are you afraid of, Emily?"

"I'm afraid of you," she whispered, her breath coming much too rapidly.

"Why?" His voice was cold. "Do you think I rescued you from that jerk just so I could take over from him myself? With my daughter asleep in the next room?"

"No. I—I don't know." She curled her fingers into her palms, remembering the giggling Vera and her angry husband. Tommy's presence hadn't seemed to make much difference then.

"Oh, don't you? Well, I can assure you that I don't have rape in mind every time I kiss a pretty woman."

"No," said Emily wearily, eyeing the large hands resting on his thighs with trepidation. "I think you have compliance in mind, haven't you? Enthusiastic compliance."

Aaron responded with one very succinct word, turned his back, and strode across to the window. "Who the hell do you think I am?" he demanded, ripping back the curtain and facing out into the night. "Don Juan? Bluebeard? Genghis Khan?"

"No, just a man with an arrogant conviction of his own irresistibility."

She didn't really want to insult him, but it seemed the safest way to hold him at bay. If he knew for one moment how close she had come to complete capitulation there would be no stopping him. Aaron was undoubtedly a man of lusty, albeit indiscriminate appetites.

He whirled around then, leaning back with his hands pressed behind him on the sill. "Right," he ground out. "And since I'm so convinced I'm irresistible, I'm not likely to take no for an answer, am I? So I suggest we adjourn to the sofa next door."

Emily's eyes widened in alarm and she took a hasty step backward.

"Oh, go to bed, Emily," he growled, black eyes snapping. When she only gasped, he added in a tone that grated like gravel under the wheels of a truck, "*Alone*. I may just survive the disappointment."

Emily, needing no second invitation, made a beeline for her bedroom and locked the door.

A few minutes later, as she sat on the edge of the big bed and tried to remove her shoes without waking Tommy, she remembered she hadn't visited the bathroom.

Feeling like a complete fool, she stepped out into the small hallway and glanced anxiously into the kitchen. Aaron wasn't there. She darted into the bathroom.

When she came out he was lounging in the entrance to the living room with his shirt off and his arms crossed magisterially on his chest.

"Better move it, Little Red Riding Hood," he taunted, as she scurried past. "The Big Bad Wolf may get you yet."

She moved it, and quickly shut the door.

Damn him, she thought, as she pulled the covers up to her chin. How in the world had a day that had started out as an interesting but ordinary excursion managed to end up like this? And why was she feeling guilty that she'd been less than polite to Aaron? True, he had rescued her from a very unpleasant situation, but yesterday he had also been all set to take advantage of the availability of another man's wife. If she, Emily, had been willing, he'd have taken advantage of her too, Tommy or no Tommy.

She closed her eyes, expecting that, as usual, David's beloved face would appear in front of her in the darkness. But tonight, for the first time in years, it didn't come.

She shifted her head on the pillow and listened to the faint rustle of the wind in the trees. What was happening to her? She always saw David...

Aaron. It must have something to do with Aaron. She groaned. Not content with disrupting her orderly existence, was he also about to disrupt her sleep? Again?

Not if she could help it.

Closing her eyes once more, she wondered if confusion and irritation would keep her awake in spite of her resolution. But they didn't. Instead, as she drifted into a restless sleep, she was conscious not of David's absence from her dreams, nor of her frightening encounter with the jerk. Instead, she found herself remembering her war of words with Aaron after that peculiarly dreamlike kiss... and she experienced a curious sense of regret...

"Emily, there's some kind of animal in the house."

"Mmm?" Emily opened a bleary eye, to find Tommy leaning over the brass bed with her soft beige hair falling across her face and her eyes very big and concerned.

"An animal. There's something snuffling at the bedroom door. D'you s'pose it's a raccoon? Or..." her eyes grew even bigger "...a skunk?"

"Not very likely," said Emily, coming fully awake and sitting up. She listened, and the snuffling turned into excited panting. "As a matter of fact, it sounds like Biscuit."

"Biscuit?" Tommy blinked.

"My dog. My neighbor's been looking after him and Buster. He probably saw my car and let them in."

"Don't you lock the front door?" asked Tommy. "On our street back home in Boston, everybody locks their doors."

"So do I," admitted Emily, as something soft bumped against the wall. "Living this far back in the woods I'd be foolish not to. But Andrew has a key for emergencies."

"Oh, I see," said Tommy, satisfied. "Is it all right if I let Biscuit in, then?"

"Sure."

Three seconds later Emily was flattened against the pillows as two large paws descended onto her chest, and a wet black nose began to investigate her face. Eventually, having satisfied itself that the face was as it should be, the nose removed itself and two big fawn-colored paws thudded to their rightful place on the floor.

"He's cute," said Tommy. "Kind of different. What sort of dog is he?"

"A very good question to which there's no rational answer," replied Emily, grinning. "I *think* he was the result of an accident between a German shepherd and a woolly mammoth."

Tommy laughed. "You're funny," she announced, running a pensive eye over the accident in question, who was now scratching vigorously at an ear that had given up the battle to point upward, and flopped over at the top in a soft curl. "He does look a bit woolly in parts," she added. "Around his feet and down the front of his chest. The rest of him's all smooth and soft, though."

Emily smiled. "Yes, he's a bit of a muddle, isn't he? The animal shelter was relieved to find him a home."

Tommy regarded her solemnly. "You're kind too," she declared. "I didn't really mean what I said yesterday—about Dad kissing you, and about his girlfriends and the Ugly Duckling and all that."

"No," said Emily faintly, "I didn't think you did. Er—why *do* you say things you don't mean, Tommy?"

"I don't know." Tommy pulled at the neck of her nightgown. "I guess I was just mad at Dad 'cos he said I could only have one chocolate bar. Then you were so nice about my hair and everything—and I felt bad."

Emily smiled. "Never mind, there's no harm done, so let's forget about it. Can we be friends?"

Tommy beamed at her. "Yes, I——"

Her words were cut short, as a stentorian bellow thundered from somewhere outside the door, shattering the early morning peace, and causing Biscuit to dive for cover beneath the bed.

"What the *hell*...?" roared a familiar baritone, as Tommy and Emily, after exchanging startled glances, pulled on their robes and hurried out into the hall.

Aaron was standing in the entrance to the living room, his finger pointed accusingly at a white, short-haired cat with green, part Siamese eyes. A cat who was seated comfortably on a brown woolen object which was spread over a small green velvet chair.

"Oh, dear," said Emily, deciding that the brown object was probably a sweater belonging to Aaron, and wishing her pet would stop performing his morning wash-and-brush-up on her guest's property. "Sorry, but Buster always sleeps in that chair."

"Well, he wasn't in it when I left my clothes there last night," growled Aaron, scowling fiercely.

"No, because he was over at Andrew's. He..." She stopped, as it was dawned on her that her pulse rate would be greatly reduced if the garment that was causing all the trouble was on its owner's back instead of under her cat. With bare feet, a bare chest covered in fine, silky dark hair, and with his jeans unbelted and hanging precariously low on his hips, Aaron Silverstone was an altogether inspiring sight. Much too inspiring.

"I'll rescue it for you," she said quickly, darting past him to lift an indignant Buster from his perch. She picked up the sweater and held it out to Aaron, trying not to let her eyes sink lower than his chin.

"Thanks so much," he muttered sarcastically. "For your information, I could have rousted that furry feline myself. The problem isn't the damn cat. The problem, in case you hadn't noticed, is hair. Cat hair. *White* cat hair. All over my *brown* sweater."

Emily sighed. He really was being unreasonable. And after the way he'd behaved last night she couldn't imagine why he thought she should give a damn about his sweater. "I'll have it dry-cleaned," she said woodenly. "Will that do?"

To her surprise, Aaron's bad-tempered scowl vanished as if it had never existed, and he smiled with suspicious meekness. "I guess it might," he said, tilting his head to one side and surveying her with frank speculation. "That'll take a few days, though, won't it?"

Oh. That explained the speculation. In spite of what he'd said last night, as he had no particular schedule to follow Aaron thought he perceived an opportunity to hang around Cinnamon Bay trying to overcome her resistance to his formidable charm.

"It will take *one* day," she said firmly. "I'll pick it up tomorrow and send it along to you by mail."

"No need for that. I'll stay on and check out the tourist potential in these parts."

"No need for that either," she said quickly. "We have golf, fishing, swimming, one inn, three motels—and that's it."

"Nonetheless, I'd like to take a look for myself." He smiled, outclassing Buster by a mile in the cat-that-swallowed-the-canary department.

Emily recognized bulldozer tactics when she saw them, and suspected she'd been outmaneuvered.

"Where are you expecting to stay?" she asked, keeping her gaze riveted on the cleft in his chin.

He didn't answer, and, in the end, Tommy was the cause of her undoing.

"Can't we stay here?" she asked, oblivious to the tensions swirling in the air about her. "You've got a neat little house, Emily, just like in a fairy tale, with the woods around it and everything. And I don't have a cat or dog at home because Mrs. Krowiak, our housekeeper, is kind of old, and she's scared of animals." When Emily swallowed and said nothing, she went on quickly, "Dad's always a grouch in the mornings, but he really doesn't mind cats."

"You, my girl, had better watch your tongue, or you'll find out just how big a grouch I can be," said Aaron threateningly.

But Tommy only giggled.

Mrs. Krowiak, Emily was thinking. So there was definitely no new Mrs. Silverstone? Aaron had not been misleading her.

She started, as she saw that both Tommy and her father were waiting expectantly for an answer—Tommy eagerly, her father smugly.

"I guess you can stay," she agreed weakly.

What the hell, Emily thought, staring resignedly at the two triumphant faces. When it came right down to it, she felt a surprising affection for unattractive, outspoken little Tommy—and surely she could put up with her difficult father for one more day? Provided he intended to get dressed. She cleared her throat. "I'll whip up something for breakfast while you put your clothes on," she said to Aaron, tightening the belt of her robe and turning away.

"What are you planning to whip up?" he asked, not troubling to hide his uneasiness.

"You'll see." Picking up Buster, she hurried out into the hall.

"That's what I'm afraid of," he shouted after her.

But Emily had already gone.

She dressed hastily in jeans and a blue top, fed Buster and Biscuit, who were both in the kitchen looking hopeful, and wondered what she could serve her guests to eat.

"Are we having eggs?" asked Tommy, wandering in and making directly for Buster.

"Not if the Lord is truly merciful," muttered Aaron, who was right behind her.

Emily turned around to glare, and saw that he was wearing a maroon sweatshirt on top of his jeans. Thank goodness for that. "We can have pancakes if you like," she said coldly.

"Can you cook pancakes?"

"Can you?" Emily put her hands on her hips.

"I thought you'd never ask!" With a speed that took her breath away, he crossed the floor, took her by the arms, and planted her down at the table.

"Sit," he ordered. "Breakfast is on me. Provided I can find anything in this mess." He pulled open a cupboard door, discovered it was almost empty, and slammed it shut.

"The flour is right there in that canister," said Emily in her best duchess voice.

"That's a canister?" Aaron picked up an oversize pickle jar and shook his head.

Emily tightened her lips and said nothing.

After much clattering and whisking, but in a surprisingly short space of time, he was placing a plateful of fluffy golden pancakes in front of her.

They tasted and smelled wonderful, like warm gold sunshine, and when he unearthed a bottle of maple syrup that she was sure she'd finished weeks ago Emily thought she'd died and gone to heaven. With her mouth full of pancake, and Aaron urging her to eat more, it was impossible to maintain the frigid politeness with which she'd planned to carry the day. Frigidity wasn't an option in the face of his persistently engaging good humor. The roaring bad temper of half an hour ago was as if it had never happened, and the wolf of the night before had vanished too. It was hard to remember he'd existed.

"Tommy says you come from Boston," she said brightly, deciding to make polite overtures and satisfy her curiosity at the same time. "What brought you all the way up here?"

"I thought I told you. Travel's my business."

"Yeah, Dad owns a big company," chipped in Tommy. "But in the summer we always get to travel ourselves, 'cos Dad doesn't really like offices. He used to be a prospector, but he stopped when my mother died. He says he doesn't mind, but I think he does." She threw a keen glance at her father, who lifted his hand to ruffle her silky hair.

"I don't mind," he assured her. "I wouldn't want my favorite daughter to grow up trailing around the backwoods after me. Especially not when she has just about every allergy known to woman."

Emily felt a quick flare of sympathy for this man who had apparently given up the life he loved for his daughter. When he wasn't going out of his way to drive her crazy, Aaron Silverstone did have his good points.

After that, conversation flowed easily and, mainly because of Tommy's ingenuous interruptions, by the time they had finished breakfast Emily had learned quite a lot about Aaron and his odd little daughter.

She discovered that Aaron loved horses and hated dancing, that his parents had died from the complications of flu when Tommy was two, that he had no brothers or sisters, and that the two of them lived with their widowed housekeeper in a large white house on a hill. She also discovered that Tommy was an "A" student in school, and that Aaron was thirty-five years old.

"Much too old to be going out with girlfriends," said Tommy, giving her father a very pointed look. "Unless he's going to marry one, of course." She sighed. "If he did, I probably wouldn't like her."

"Wouldn't you?" said Emily, gulping, and avoiding Aaron's eye as she stirred two lumps of sugar—which she didn't take—into a steaming cup of black coffee.

"I don't think so," sighed Tommy, licking a crumb off her chin. "'Course, he hasn't had many lately. And it was different when he went out with Marabel. She just lived down the street and we were friends. But she went away. To study art in Paris, Dad said, but Mrs. Krowiak said it wasn't art she went to study, it was——"

"That'll do, Tommy," Aaron interrupted, in the sort of voice no one in their right mind would disobey. "I'm sure Emily isn't interested in Marabel, any more than she is in the dreary details of my social life."

No, thought Emily, closing her eyes. She certainly *wasn't* interested in the Marabel side of his life, but, with a face and physique like he had, she was willing to bet it was anything but dreary.

"How long have you been alone?" she asked him, more to take his steely eye off Tommy than because it mattered to her. Then she glanced at his face and wished she hadn't brought the subject up.

Two narrow lines distorted the flat line of his mouth, and his eyes were as hard as black marble. When she looked away, she saw that he had picked up a knife, and was holding it as if it were a weapon.

"You could say I've always been alone," he said harshly. "But if you mean how long has it been since Tommy's mother died, the answer is nine years."

"Yes, and I don't even remember her," said Tommy, not sounding as if she cared much. Then her eyes clouded. "Grandma gave me a picture of her, though. She was beautiful. Not like me."

"Cut it out, Tommy." Aaron's response was automatic. Then he added abruptly, "But if you really want to know, you're far more beautiful than she was. In ways that matter."

Tommy sighed. "You're just being nice, Dad. You know it's not true. Grandma said so, even though she didn't mean me to hear." She sighed again. "I wish my mother hadn't called me Thomasina, though."

"So do I," said Aaron, his features softening a little as he looked down at his daughter.

Emily frowned. There were undercurrents here she didn't understand. If Aaron had had the good sense not to choose Tommy's name, why on earth had he allowed it to be foisted on her? He didn't seem the sort of man who would give in on a subject like that without a fight. It didn't sound as though his marriage had been a particularly happy one either, she decided. Perhaps that was why he had contented himself with the Veras of the world since his wife died.

"I'm sorry," she said now, feeling that she'd committed some terrible *faux pas*, but not quite knowing what it was. "Perhaps I shouldn't have asked..."

"Perhaps you shouldn't." He put the knife down very deliberately and leaned back, toying with the handle of his cup. "But you did, and now it's my turn. What's a beautiful woman like you doing buried back here in the bush? Unhappy love affair?"

Emily gasped. "No, certainly not!" she said indignantly. "I bought this place three years ago from a girl called Belinda because I wanted a change of pace. I lived in Victoria then, and I met her when she married Hal Blake, the bicycle man, and moved down there. Then she had two daughters, and decided to sell her old home to me. It's worked out perfectly..." She paused, because she'd run out of steam.

"Mmm-hmm." His mouth canted at one corner. "As a matter of fact I wasn't asking for the details of your real-estate transactions. Why did you want a change of pace, Emily?" His eyes bored into her like twin arrows, forcing her to face the memories that she had spent the last six years of her life trying desperately not to confront.

"I had to get away," she replied evasively.

"So do I," interrupted Tommy, giggling. "Excuse me, please, but can I go out and play with Biscuit?"

"He'd love you to."

The reprieve only lasted a minute. After Tommy and Biscuit had departed in a flurry of fur and blue jeans, Aaron rested an arm on the table, fixed Emily with a commanding eye, and repeated, "Yes? You had to get away from what?"

She noticed the muscles flex in his forearm, stared at the corded sinews of his neck, thought despairingly of another neck and other muscular forearms—and said in a voice so low that Aaron couldn't catch it, "I don't want to talk about it now."

"What was that?"

Oh, God, he hadn't heard her. And his eyes were as daunting as those of a lawyer demanding confirmation of a crime. She didn't have to answer him, of course. There was no earthly reason why she should, and he had no right to demand information, but...

Quite suddenly, and for no apparent reason, her resistance crumbled. The reticence she had maintained in the face of well-meant inquiries, not to mention downright nosiness, for the last six years, was swept away by an urgent, overpowering need to confide in—of all people—this arrogant, unreasonable, utterly magnetic man she had known for two days. It made no sense, but gradually, stumbling over the words, she admitted, "I was getting away from my—memories." She put an elbow on the table and covered her face with a hand.

"Sometimes it's necessary to face one's memories, Emily. Otherwise, in the end, they'll destroy you."

Aaron spoke with such quiet authority that, at least for this moment, she believed him. "Yes," she said. "Yes, perhaps..." She stopped, swallowed. "I—you see... No, of course you don't." She started again. "I was married—in Victoria. Six years ago, when I was twenty-two. I married my childhood sweetheart, and we had a big wedding and a wonderful honeymoon in Greece. When we came back we moved into our own little home. For me there'd never been anyone but David, and I don't even remember falling in love because it seemed as though I'd always loved him. But we'd only been married three months..." She rubbed a knuckle across her eyes, then stared at it, puzzled because it came away wet. "Three months... And then I came home from shopping one Saturday afternoon—and I found him."

"Found him?" Aaron's voice was calm, steadying.

"He had an aneurism, in his head." Now that she had spoken the words, they didn't seem so unbearable any more. "We didn't know about it. He was lying on the kitchen floor, with a peanut-butter sandwich beside him. And he was dead."

CHAPTER FOUR

EMILY was staring straight through Aaron, not seeing the maroon sweatshirt any more, unaware of the quiet compassion in his eyes. Instead she saw a tiled floor, white with gray flecks, the small bruise on David's temple where he had hit his head when he fell...

"Emily," said Aaron, his voice penetrating the pain that was as raw as it had always been. "Emily, you have to learn to deal with the past, to put it behind you. Otherwise you'll never have a future."

She looked at him then, startled not so much by his tone as by his words. She might have known Aaron wouldn't offer easy sympathy, predictable platitudes. And she was grateful.

"How did you guess?" she asked, her eyes clouded.

"Guess?"

"Yes. About me—about the memories never going away for very long." She swallowed, and when he only stared at her, his eyes giving nothing away, she added, shakily, "Aaron, you know, don't you, that I've been running away all this time? Why—how did you——?"

"Because I've been there."

Emily jumped, her fingers rattling the spoon in her cup. Aaron wasn't speaking calmly now. His voice had come out cracked and rasping, and the line of his mouth was hard.

"You mean you—ran away too?" she whispered.

"No, but I wanted to—how I wanted to!" He crushed his napkin into a limp rag and slapped it onto the table.

"In the end, though, I knew I had to face up to what I'd done. Even though I hadn't known I was doing it."

Emily stared into her cup. The coffee was cold now, black and unappetizing. There was a small smear of pink on the rim. This was an aspect of Aaron she hadn't even considered. An Aaron who wasn't always the Inquisitor, who wasn't always arrogantly in control, making her think of things that were better forgotten. She sighed softly, accepting the fact that maybe, deep down, she had felt a certain empathy with this abrasive man right from the beginning. Maybe that was why, after living in Cinnamon Bay for three years, he was the only person she had talked to about David's death. Even Yvonne, her good friend, knew only that she was widowed.

"What did you want to run away from?" she asked now, lifting her gaze from the coffee, trying not to think of her dead husband.

"It doesn't matter. I've paid my debts, Emily. It's you we're talking about now."

Yes, she thought, he might have paid his debts, whatever they were. But some residue of the past was still with him. Perhaps he hadn't really got over the—pain. Because it *was* pain she had heard behind the abrasive rasp. She glanced quickly at his set features, but he was the Chieftain again now, his face unreadable, impassive.

"You know about guilt too, don't you?" she said quietly. "My guilt, I mean."

"I suspected."

She ran a finger absently around the edge of her plate. "I thought so. Is that why you're talking to me as no one, except my mother, has ever had the nerve to talk before? Is that why you're asking questions you've no right to ask?'

Aaron slung an arm over the back of his chair and leaned backward. "I'm damned if I know," he admitted wryly. "But I do know that if you don't face up to things, Emily, you'll never be a whole woman."

"What things?" she asked, with instant suspicion. She wasn't sure if she wanted to be a "whole woman". That sounded too much like self-interest—on his part.

"Things like not being there when it happened. Like thinking that if you had been you could have saved him. The same unprofitable muddle of 'what-ifs' that we're all prone to."

When she only stared silently, he nodded, and added on an almost casual note, "I see. You'd quarreled with him, had you?"

Hostility churned inside her and boiled up to the surface. "What do you know about it?" she demanded, leaping angrily to her feet. "Yes, sure we'd had words. About a *cat*, of all things. I wanted one of the neighbor's kittens, and he didn't. He wouldn't even consider it, and I was hurt and disappointed, so I stormed off to spend our hard-earned money on clothes I didn't want." She turned her back on him and started slamming dishes into the sink. "I said some things I didn't mean—and he just laughed. That made me even angrier. Later, when I'd calmed down, I remembered that David always laughed when he didn't know what else to do. It was one of the things about him that I loved. And I knew he was half afraid of cats. So I went home. And he was there—he—he…" She dropped the cup she was holding. It fell against the edge of the counter and broke, missing the water.

Emily stared at the shattered crumbs of china, her hands curled around the edge of the sink. And then she felt her shoulders shaking. They didn't seem to belong to her, and she didn't know how to stop them. She couldn't see the broken cup any more either, because her eyes were misted with tears that were as gray as the dirty dishwater.

Blindly, not seeing Buster sitting hopefully at her feet, she turned away and stumbled toward the door—or where she imagined the door must be.

Buster let out a screech of protest, and as Emily's vision cleared, she saw him jump indignantly onto the table to join the remains of breakfast. At the same time two strong arms came around her from behind. Then she was being turned around, pressed against a hard male body. It was a warm body, tough and reassuring. And she fitted against it as if it were where she belonged.

"I've done it again, haven't I?" she heard Aaron mutter, more or less to himself.

"Done what?" she sniffed, liking the softness of his sweatshirt beneath her cheek.

"Made you cry."

That jolted her from the mindless euphoria that had followed the catharsis of anger, and she put both hands on his chest and pushed herself out of his embrace.

"You must think that's all I ever do," she said listlessly, keeping her eyes fixed steadfastly around the region of his navel.

He shook his head. "No. Why should I think that? Last night you suffered an experience that would make most women with imagination cry. And this morning—this morning I forced you to face something I suspect you've been successfully not facing for years. Am I right?"

Emily lifted her head, to deny it, but from somewhere on the perimeter of her vision she saw Buster's paw reach out to bat the open bottle of syrup on the table.

"Hey!" she shouted. "Cut it out, Buster!"

In the same moment as she made a dive for the cat, she caught a glimpse of Aaron's face, saw his eyebrows go up, and heard him mutter, "Buster? Who the hell do you think you're calling...?"

Then she heard no more, as the syrup hit the table, and the cat gave her a green-eyed stare before jumping in dignified slow motion to the floor. Emily groaned, and uttered one short, expressive phrase.

"Mind your language in front of my daughter," drawled Aaron's dry voice from behind her.

"Why?" That was Tommy's voice. "You never mind *your* language, Dad. When we nearly missed the boat because I stayed too long in the washroom yesterday, you said——"

"Never mind what I said," growled her father. "Emily, are you all right?"

Somehow she knew he didn't mean was it all right that there was syrup all over the table, and that she was having a sticky time of it with a paper towel.

"Yes," she said quietly, surprised to find that she meant it. "You know, I really think I may be just fine." She straightened, turning to face him with a faint frown creasing her brow. "I—it hurt to talk about it, but I'm glad I did. Thank you."

He gave her a lopsided smile that did something unexpected to her knees. "Don't mention it. I've always fancied myself as a knight in shining armor, but unfortunately my knight-errantry rarely works out the way it's supposed to."

Emily frowned, wondering if he meant that his damsels in distress didn't always fall gratefully into his bed. "I didn't mean thank you for yesterday," she said.

"Neither did I." He smiled again, so explicitly, and with such potent effect, that Emily veered away to concentrate all her attention on the sticky table.

"Dad," said Tommy disgustedly, "you talk an awful lot of baloney. You're a travel consultant, not a knight. But I suppose you think it'll make Emily let you kiss her, just like you used to kiss Marabel when you talked baloney."

"Tommy," said Aaron, pleasantly but with total finality, "I kissed Marabel goodbye—once—when she refused to let me rescue her from the clutches of a particularly persistent gentleman from Paris. And if you open your mouth again for the next half-hour, I shall take great pleasure in gagging it with one of Emily's dish towels. Assuming I can find one. Failing that, sticky paper towel will do as well."

Tommy giggled. "You're nuts," she said cheerfully. "I'm going to play with Biscuit."

"Thank heaven for another small mercy," muttered Aaron as she scampered out of the kitchen.

Emily looked up at him doubtfully. "Was Marabel one of your failed attempts at knight-errantry?" she inquired, wondering if he would chew her out for asking, and feeling a certain amount of surprise that this self-assured man could actually fail in anything he put his mind to. Especially anything female.

"Not in the way you mean. We were friends. I'd known her since she was a kid, and she wasn't much more than that when she left for France."

"To study art?"

"Not really. Mrs. Krowiak was right about that. I think she had studies of a rather more biological nature in mind." His voice was as dry as dead leaves.

Emily choked, and Aaron eyed her sardonically. "You find studies of that nature amusing, do you?" he murmured. "It seems we have more in common than I thought."

Emily gulped, and returned hastily to the sink. "No," she mumbled, with her back to him, "I don't. At least—I mean..." She took a deep breath and started again. "I don't teach biology," she managed finally.

Behind her she heard an explosive snort, then Aaron muttered something that sounded like, "I'm relieved to hear it."

She thought about turning around to throw her wet dishrag in his mocking face, but in the end she decided that dignified indifference was the best policy, and continued doggedly on with the dishes. She knew Aaron was watching her, and she could sense his dark eyes admiring a part of her which was no particular business of his. But when she spun around to confront him he had gone.

As soon as she finished, she dried her hands and hurried outside.

"And where do you think you're going?" asked Aaron, who was leaning up against a tree watching Tommy gambol about with Biscuit on a patch of grass.

"To see Andrew," she replied shortly.

"Andrew?" His eyes narrowed.

"My neighbor. He's been looking after my animals."

"Ah. I'll escort you."

"No, you won't."

"Why not? Is Andrew private property? Yours, for instance?" The cool drawl had a faintly malicious ring to it.

"No, of course not..."

"Good. Then let's be on our way." He peeled himself away from the tree and came toward her, pulling her arm through his in a gesture of intimate possession.

She threw him an exasperated glance and shrugged irritably, annoyed to find that she liked the feel of his thigh touching her hip. "What about Tommy?" she asked.

"Tommy!" he called, jerking his head at his daughter. "Come on, we're going to visit Emily's boyfriend."

"He is not my boyfriend," hissed Emily, as Tommy came skipping up to them, followed by Biscuit.

"No? What is he, then?" enquired Aaron, not sounding as if he believed her.

"He's Andrew Hatton, the artist. You've probably never heard of him," she said loftily.

"As a matter of fact, I have. I'm not totally ignorant of the art world. The man has quite a reputation. In more ways than one," he added, with a slight curl of his lip. "I think I'm beginning to see..."

"There's nothing to see," snapped Emily. But Aaron was still holding her arm, and after a moment she decided there was no point in engaging in an undignified scuffle. Tilting her nose in the air, she started to move off down the lane. Aaron, noting the angle of her nose, tightened his grip and made no effort to suppress a crooked smile.

Even before they reached the small clearing in front of a cottage very similar to Emily's, the door was flung open by a big, piratical-looking man who obviously hadn't shaved for several days.

"Emily, my love!" he shouted, throwing wide his arms. "Wonderful to see you again! Come and give your favorite neighbor a kiss."

Emily gritted her teeth. Andrew *would* go into his lover-boy act at the most inopportune moment he could pick.

"Hello, Andrew," she muttered, staring studiously at her sandaled feet. "How are you?"

"All the better for seeing you." He swaggered out onto the step and gave her a broad, unabashedly wolfish grin. "Where have you been, love? I knew you were back, and when I let the animals in I saw a strange car parked..." He broke off and made a great production of appearing to take in Aaron's presence for the first time. "Aha—I *see*," he continued. "Been cheating on me, have you?" He turned a speculative but not noticeably perturbed eye on his alleged rival, who was standing next to Emily with his arm draped casually over her shoulder, affecting an air of faintly bored uninterest.

"Andrew!" moaned Emily. "For heaven's sake stop it!"

"Stop what, love?"

"Stop trying to make it sound as if—as if we..." She ran a hand helplessly through her hair and pulled away from Aaron's easy embrace. "Just stop it, that's all. I only came to thank you for taking care of Buster and Biscuit. It was kind of you."

"Any time. But I'd much rather take care of you."

"Andrew, please." Emily took a deep breath, and managed to get a grip on the situation. "Aaron, this is Andrew Hatton. He moved in here just a few weeks after I came to Cinnamon Bay."

"How convenient," drawled Aaron, not acknowledging the introduction.

Emily glared at him. "And, Andrew, this is Aaron Silverstone. He did me a—a favor. And he couldn't find anywhere to stay."

"Equally convenient," murmured Andrew, ignoring the conventions as well, and throwing a blatantly derisive glance at Aaron.

"It is *not* convenient," snapped Emily. Then she saw Tommy watching her with big, troubled eyes, and added quickly, "I haven't introduced you to Tommy. What I mean is, I'm happy to be able to help Aaron and his *daughter* out." She placed extra emphasis on the "daughter" in the hopes of disabusing Andrew of the idea that she was enjoying a private little love tryst with her guest.

"Ah, I see—a chaperone. Never mind, love, I'm sure you've found a way——"

"Unfortunately she hasn't," interrupted Aaron, pushing his hands into his pockets and lifting his head to stare with undisguised contempt at the other man. "No doubt you've had better luck. I congratulate you. Emily, I'll leave you and your friend to celebrate your homecoming in private."

"Aaron!" she cried, resenting the sneer in his voice, and not sure at this moment whether she wanted to fling her arms about him and drag him back, or administer a carefully placed kick to his departing, but still maddeningly beguiling backside.

In the end she did neither, because he had already disappeared into the trees, and Andrew was watching her with a knowing smile on his rather too fleshy lips. She could tell that, although he didn't really give a damn whom she slept with, he was now turning over the possibility that the hitherto unobtainable Emily might not be so unobtainable after all.

Like his cottage's previous owner, who at the ripe age of seventy-one had suddenly upped, married and moved to Victoria, Andrew was a fairly successful artist. But whereas old Joe McIlwain had been a kindly curmudgeon, Andrew Hatton was a shameless sensualist. He was pleasant enough company when he wanted to be, but he had never let up on his campaign to lure his attractive neighbor into his bed. Emily knew he was perfectly harmless, or she would not have trusted him with her key. But she could certainly have done without the incentive that Aaron's presence would undoubtedly add to Andrew's already persistent offensive.

"Honestly, Andrew," she groaned now, "did you *have* to do that?"

This time he didn't pretend not to understand her. "No, of course not. But I enjoyed it. Serves you right for not coming over to thank me for looking after your pets. You might have told me you were back, love."

"Yes, I'm sorry, but it was late, and something rather awful had happened. I came as soon as we finished breakfast..."

"Apart from which, you were having a nice little party with your handsome friend." His slightly decadent mouth parted in a suggestive leer. "Don't blame you, love. As long as he hasn't stolen all the fire."

"There wasn't any fire," said Emily, suddenly tired of this scene. "And I don't care whether you believe me or not, Andrew. Now, if you don't mind, I have to be going. I've got a lot to do this morning."

"I don't doubt it. Lucky—what did you say the fellow's name was? Aaron?"

"Andrew!" Emily started to remonstrate, then thought better of it. What was the point? "Thanks again," she said curtly.

"Is that the best you can do?" he asked, feigning offense. "Not even a kiss?"

She was about to tell him what she thought of that suggestion when she saw he was laughing at her, so in the end she just shrugged and gave up. Andrew had always been incorrigible. It wasn't likely he would change now, just because she happened to have a house guest.

"Not even a kiss," she said, turning away with a tired smile. "See you soon, Andrew."

She walked briskly off into the trees without bothering to wait for his answer.

Aaron's head was buried in the inner workings of the station wagon when she got back. Emily stopped for a moment to admire the view. Very nice, she decided. Just the sort of male backside she liked. Taut, enticingly upthrust... Then she sat on the thought quickly as he stood up, wiping his hands on a rag.

"Trouble?" she asked politely, as if the scene in front of Andrew's cottage hadn't happened.

"Nope. Just checking," he said tersely. "What happened to your artistic friend? That was a very brief reunion celebration."

"It wasn't a celebration," said Emily crossly. "Not that it's any of your business. Now, if it's all the same to you, I think I'll just take your sweater in to the cleaners."

"You'll also take your tire to the garage."

"Who says?" demanded Emily, fighting a childish urge to stick out her tongue.

"I do. Come along, we'll all go. After which you can show me the local beauty spots."

"What if I have other plans?"

"Change them." The curl of his lip had a certain arrogant charm. His gaze was cool and compelling.

Abruptly, and much to her disgust, Emily felt her defenses crumbling as a long-suppressed hunger flamed up and burned achingly inside her.

"All right," she agreed grudgingly. "We can take a picnic to Cameron Lake, if you like. Tommy would probably enjoy it."

"Mmm, she probably would. And it may disappoint you to hear that I might too."

"It doesn't disappoint me in the least," she said stiffly. Although she wasn't about to admit it, the truth of the matter was that the prospect of an afternoon in the sun with Aaron was remarkably appealing, in spite of the fact that at the back of her mind she had an idea she ought to be avoiding his company. It was dangerous. Instinctively she felt he could hurt her. Just when, for the first time in years, the burden of regret had somehow lifted. Then she shrugged the presentiment off, deciding that since she would have to put up with his presence until tomorrow, come what might, there was no reason why she shouldn't enjoy it. And in any case he lived thousands of miles away. That had to make him reasonably safe. She couldn't possibly get hurt from long distance.

Surprisingly, this conclusion wasn't quite as reassuring as she'd hoped.

Tommy was restless as a cricket on the drive out to Cameron Lake, jumping about in the back seat and every three minutes demanding to be told if they were there. "And we ought to have brought Biscuit," she announced suddenly, as they rounded a sharp curve in the road. "Can we go back for him?"

"We cannot," said Aaron shortly. "Cat fur on my sweater is one thing. Dog fur all over my car is quite another."

"We can take Emily's car, then," said Tommy, not seeing the problem. "She won't mind."

"No, but I will."

Emily glanced up at him, frowning. "What's that supposed to mean?" she asked, remembering his strictures on her driving.

"Merely that I haven't the slightest intention of driving miles back down the highway to collect yet another load on the organization," he replied flatly. "Tommy's quite enough to be going on with, and I see no reason to waste a beautiful day."

"Oh." Emily relapsed into silence, deciding there wasn't much point in arguing with that, particularly as she herself hadn't considered bringing Biscuit for precisely the reasons he'd mentioned. She listened to Tommy grumbling in the back, and reflected that it *was* a beautiful day. Yesterday's rain had left a fresh, clean smell in the air, and the sun flickering down through the evergreens was bright and inviting.

She shook her head slightly. Who would have thought that the man she had wanted to murder yesterday morning, without even having set eyes on him, would turn out to be the first person to break through the barrier she had built around her feelings for so long?

Her mind drifted back down the years, to the struggle she had had adjusting to life without her husband, and her eventual decision to start life afresh in Cinnamon Bay. It had proved a good move, she reflected. Gradually she had learned to take pleasure in her new friends and new life-style. And now, in some mysterious way, since Aaron had made her open up to him this morning, she had a sense that perhaps she might learn to lay the past to rest.

She stole a glance at his profile. It was hard, his lips pressed together in an ungiving line, and she was reminded that her murderous inclinations had not been restricted to yesterday. She had been tempted to commit double murder this morning too...

But, in the end, the idea of Aaron and Andrew both meeting their fate at her hands was so ludicrous that she found herself grinning.

Aaron, still looking unapproachable, glanced sideways. "You look like the cat who's just swallowed the family dog," he remarked dryly. "May I share the joke?"

"I—oh, it was nothing." she said quickly. No, he certainly couldn't—or in any case most surely wouldn't—share the joke.

"Mmm." He threw her another glance, enigmatic and a little sinister, then suddenly swung the car to the left so that Emily was thrown up against him.

"Dad!" protested Tommy indignantly from the back. "You did that on purpose!"

"Did I?" replied her father equably. "What makes you think so?"

"'Cos you're mad at Emily," said Tommy with daughterly perception. "You want to scare her."

Aaron smiled, not very pleasantly. "Are you scared, Emily?" he asked, as he maneuvered the station wagon expertly around a bend.

Emily pushed herself upright. "No," she said, knowing her face was flushed, and breathless from the unexpected contact with his body. "Why should I be?" She stared resolutely at the gray curve of the road and refused to look at him.

"I've no idea," he replied dryly. "But you're biting your lip."

"That's because I'm thinking," she explained in a repressive voice which she hoped would convince him she was engaged in thoughts of a deeply philosophical nature.

It didn't.

"About me, I hope," he drawled, removing his gaze from the road to favour her with the sort of suggestive leer that would have made her want to hit him if he hadn't been driving.

"Certainly not!" She pointed her nose haughtily toward the window. Beside her, he gave a low and, she was sure, deliberately aggravating chuckle.

The beach at Cameron Lake glistened like pale gilt in the sunlight, and the sands were warm to the touch. At the edge of the trees, some distance away, a family of two parents and three children were tossing a large, inflatable ball.

"Mmm, nice," said Aaron, as Emily bent over to spread a green tartan blanket on the sand.

She straightened quickly, convinced he was not referring to the scenery.

"Wow!" exclaimed Tommy, quite clearly referring to the food as she opened the lid of the picnic cooler and began to pull out pies, drinks, sandwiches and fruit. "You've sure made a lot of stuff, Emily."

"Has she?" Aaron cocked a dubious eye at the cooler. "That's ominous."

"Why?" demanded Emily, facing him with her hands on her hips.

"No reason," he said quickly. "Er—how's the tofu?"

"I've made you egg," she replied coldly.

Aaron took a deep breath. "Wonderful," he muttered. His eyes lingered pensively on her trim figure in jeans and a turquoise shirt. "Just wonderful. So let's eat."

Before she realized what he was up to, he had taken her hands in his and was pulling her down beside him on the blanket. "There," he said, "that's better, isn't it?"

It wasn't, because he had an arm around her waist and one hand rested on her hip as he settled her comfortably against him. She could feel the heat of his body through her jeans, even though he was wearing jeans too. She tried to wriggle away, but at once his fingers splayed out, holding her tighter.

"Keep still," he whispered, bending down to brush his lips over her ear. "You don't want to make a scene in front of Tommy, do you?"

She did, especially as Tommy was already munching purposefully on the sandwiches, and appeared much more interested in the family with the ball than she was in the misbehavior of her father. But now Aaron was whispering again as he leaned across her to collect a sandwich.

"You may deprive me of a decent lunch," he murmured. "There's not much I can do about that. But I'm damned if I'm going to be deprived of anything else."

"That's what you think," hissed Emily through her teeth. "Aaron, really! Tommy——"

But at that moment Tommy turned around, wiped the last crumb of sandwich from her mouth, grabbed an apple and jumped up on to her feet. "That's Jimmy from the boat," she informed them. "And his mom and dad and his brothers." She waved in the direction of the ball-playing family and ran off across the beach without waiting for parental approval.

Emily swallowed. "She certainly isn't shy, is she?" she said, a little breathlessly because Aaron's fingers were now smoothing over her hip. "I was at her age. And Aaron, please take your hand——"

"You know, I'm surprised," he interrupted her. "These sandwiches really aren't at all bad."

"I *can* boil an egg," she replied tartly.

"Yes, so I see." His hand slid down her thigh, as he bent forward to pick up a fruit pie. "Did you make these too?" He paused with his face about two inches from her nose, so that her breasts were just touching his chest.

"No," she gasped.

"Good." He took a bite, still so close that she could feel his heart thump. "Want some?"

"No!" she gasped again, pushing his hand away as he offered her a share of the pie.

"Your loss." He sat back, allowing her to breathe again, as he polished off the remainder of his lunch with leisurely enjoyment. Then he took a long swig of juice from a plastic glass, removed her glass from her hand and planted it firmly in the sand.

"Now," he said, with the confidence of a man who knows exactly what he's doing, "let's get down to serious business."

"Business?" she croaked. "What business?"

His voice was very soft when he answered—soft, but frighteningly assured. "The business of chasing away shadows," he told her, lying back and stretching himself lazily on the green tartan blanket. "I have a feeling your friend Andrew hasn't done a proper job of that."

"It's not his business to," Emily replied automatically, gaping as Aaron linked his hands behind his head and gave her a languid, anticipatory smile. She passed her tongue across her lips, unable to take her eyes off him. Nervously her fascinated gaze traveled over the lean allure of his body, mesmerized as he shifted his shoulders and settled himself in the sand like a big, confident cat.

"Come here, Emily," he said. He held out a hand, and his dark eyes were commanding as well as inviting.

She shook her head wordlessly. Even if she had known what to say, she didn't think she would have been able to utter a sound.

Aaron's smile wasn't quite so languid now as he reached his hand slowly behind her neck, stroked it for a moment, then pulled her down so that once again her breasts were touching his chest. The rest of her lay motionless beside him, and she could feel the length of his thigh along her hip.

"Wh-what are you doing?" she whispered, her voice muffled because her lips were pressed against his neck.

"Teaching you how to feel again," he answered, running a finger gently down her spine. "Six years is a long time to go without being loved. If you have gone without."

"Of course I have. But this—isn't love," she managed to gasp, knowing that if she moved even a fraction the dam she had built to hold back all physical needs would burst open in an unstoppable wave of mindless passion. If all he wanted was to make her feel again, then he had succeeded—beyond all reason. But wanting to make love to a man because he had a come-hither smile and an impossibly seductive body had nothing whatever to do with love. Even now, with all her senses reeling, she knew that.

"Perhaps not," he replied lightly, "but it may very well do for a start." Now the finger was traveling slowly up her spine again in small circling motions.

She forced herself to remain rigid, refusing to respond to him in spite of an almost overpowering urge to melt into him, to move as she had never moved before. She couldn't pull away for fear his grip would tighten and she'd be lost. She knew she mustn't lose. There was Tommy to think of. And there had been Vera, and it was broad daylight on a public beach.

"Don't!" she cried desperately. "Aaron, please! You mustn't... Tommy..."

"I'm not going to," he said, with a brisk indifference that shocked her. "I'm well aware of my responsibilities as a father. I just wanted you to know I could."

At that her body did go limp. Partly from sheer despair, but mostly because he was probably right. And the thought appalled her.

As soon as Aaron felt the resistance go out of her, he eased her away and sat up, letting his arms hang loosely over his knees as though he hadn't a care in the world.

"What's the matter?" he asked, as his gaze fell on her fuchsia-colored face. "Afraid your large neighbor with the even larger mouth may spank you for taking up with the tourist traffic?"

"Oh, don't be ridiculous!" she snapped, not sure whether she was more angry with him or with herself. She rolled as far away from him as she could, swiped a small pile of sand off the blanket, and stared dismally at the blue sky which earlier had seemed so warm and full of promise.

"What did you do that for?" she asked furiously, after a prolonged silence. "That's no way to behave in public, with your daughter watching."

"I didn't actually do anything," he pointed out. "And my daughter is not watching. I'm watching *her*, and at the moment she's running across the sand with a beach ball, and three small boys in hot pursuit."

Emily followed his pointing finger, and saw with a flick of irritation that he was right.

"It's still no way to behave," she said frigidly. "Yesterday, on the *Uchuck*, she was worrying that if you started paying attention to me you wouldn't have any time left for her. That sounded like the voice of experience."

"It wasn't," he said shortly, no longer sounding nonchalant. He stood up in a single fluid motion and, to her consternation, began to unbuckle his belt. "It was the voice of her grandparents. She overheard them speculating about my rather unexciting love life."

"What are you doing?" yelped Emily. All of a sudden Tommy's psyche and her own resentment were non-issues, as Aaron began to slide his jeans down his thighs. Oh, no! Surely he didn't plan to take her...

"Going for a swim," he replied, his coolly neutral tone bringing her swiftly from the realms of fantasy to a public beach on a sunny afternoon. "What did you imagine? That I was preparing to make love to you? On the spot?"

Emily gulped. For a moment there, that had been exactly what she'd thought. "No, I..." She stumbled to a confused halt.

"Not that the offer isn't tempting," he went on, as if she hadn't spoken. "However, I'm afraid I'll have to postpone that pleasure—temporarily."

Emily's mouth fell open. *"Offer?"* she exclaimed. "Postpone... Well, of all the—you *are* a dreamer!" She stopped abruptly as his jeans fell to the sand, and she saw that beneath them he was wearing a brief white swimsuit. The sun, shining on his golden skin, touched his body with a fiery magic which caused her to gasp and suck in her breath. Then he moved, and there was nothing magical about him any more, only a raw, unconscious maleness. She tried to look away, but she couldn't. Her eyes refused to obey her.

Aaron smiled down at her knowingly and said very softly, "You're right, I am a dreamer. And I believe in making sure my dreams come true." Without waiting for an answer, he turned his back on her and strode swiftly across the sand to the water's edge.

She stood up slowly, her gaze riveted on his naked back, and began to peel off her own clothes.

A minute later, dressed in a neat but unrevealing black one-piece, she started across the beach behind him. The sand felt warm and comforting between her toes, and by the time she caught up with him some of her unbearable feeling of tension had drained away.

He was standing with the water lapping around his feet, and as she came up beside him, he held out his hand. Almost shyly, she took it, and side by side they waded in up to their waists.

The water was cold, a bird was chirping in a nearby tree, and Aaron's blatant sexuality wasn't quite as threatening as before. He released her hand, shouted at her to follow, and began to swim with deep, powerful strokes that soon put some distance between them. But in a moment, as she struggled to catch up, he was back. And then his hands were on her waist, towing her easily with him toward the shore. Emily lay on her back, her long auburn hair trailing in the lake, and let herself drift lazily beside him.

When they reached the shallows again, Aaron didn't release her. Instead he stood holding her lightly, as he looked her over with a small, appreciative smile.

"Very prim and proper," he said, nodding at the black one-piece. "However, I'm delighted to be able to inform you that when it's all slicked down with water like that it doesn't leave a great deal to the imagination." To emphasize his point, he ran his hands very slowly over her wet hips, and Emily gasped at the shaft of pure desire that twisted up her body in a hot coil. She gazed at him, shaken, and yet spellbound by a sexuality that was more powerful than any magnet. His body glistened with drops of pure gold, and his thick hair, plastered wetly to his face, emphasized the high, molded cheekbones that made him look like some ancient god.

"Hey!" Tommy's youthful voice shattered the spell. "Jimmy and me and the twins want to go swimming too!"

"Jimmy and I," her father corrected her, as Emily heaved a sigh of gratitude at being relieved of the necessity to respond to Aaron's gibe about her swimsuit—which in her view was entirely respectable.

After that there was no opportunity for either of them to do anything other than keep a businesslike eye on the antics of Tommy and her attendants, whose parents appeared to appreciate the respite. Several times during the course of the afternoon Emily was conscious of Aaron's gaze resting on her with cool speculation, and she thought of the evening ahead with a mixture of trepidation and resolve. Aaron could speculate all he liked, but he would find she didn't come with the board and room.

Several hours later, as evening shadows fell, they drove back to the cottage in a kind of wary silence that was not difficult to maintain this time, because Tommy, in the back seat, was half asleep.

"That was a great day," she said drowsily, as they sat in the kitchen drinking the remains of the juice. "I like being here, Emily. You're lucky." She bent down to pat an ecstatically wriggling Biscuit.

"Am I?" said Emily, smiling at the tousled little girl. "I'm glad you enjoyed it. And now I suppose we'd better have some supper.

"I'm tired," mumbled Tommy, yawning. "Can't I just have a glass of milk?"

Emily looked questioningly at Aaron, who shrugged and said that, as the alternative was probably oat bran or overcooked eggs, milk might not be a bad idea.

Emily aimed a deliberate kick at his shins, but he only laughed and dodged expertly out of the line of fire.

Not long afterward, with Tommy quietly sleeping off the effects of her busy day, Aaron and Emily sat down to wine and a plateful of grilled cheese sandwiches. When Aaron pronounced them merely tolerable, Emily tossed her head and told him he ought to be grateful, because the alternative was soy beans on toast.

He shuddered.

Later, when the two of them moved into the living room to drink their coffee, Emily was quick to occupy the small green velvet chair that earlier had been occupied by Buster—and Aaron's sweater.

Aaron lowered himself on to the Regency-striped sofa, and fastened his eyes on her in the way she imagined a snake with a sense of humor might watch its prey. "A wise choice," he murmured.

She blinked. "What?"

"A wise choice. That charming but inadequate chair that couldn't possibly support two people."

"Well, I hope not. Why should it?" Emily was irritated. This room, with its muted blues and greens, and the delicate pastel prints she had chosen to hang on the walls, usually had a soothing effect on her. But its magic wasn't working this evening.

"No reason at all," Aaron replied smoothly, swallowing a mouthful of coffee. "Mmm, this is very good."

"I'm glad I can do something right," she snapped, still irritated, and wishing she didn't feel like a blushing teenager whenever Aaron paid her a compliment. Really, it was extraordinary the effect he had on her. It seemed to be a combination of acute, semi-permanent exasperation, and pure lust. Both of which emotions she could do without.

"Tommy seemed quite different today," she said, in an effort to take her mind off the long body draped sexily over her sedate striped sofa. "Yesterday she was all spiky and suspicious. Today she's just a happy little girl."

To her surprise, his expression changed, and she sensed an instant withdrawal. "Tommy's all right," he said gruffly. "The spikes usually disappear once I get her back."

"From her grandparents?" Emily asked doubtfully.

"Right." The one-word answer came out like a military marching order.

She frowned. "I don't understand. If they upset her like that, why do you allow her to visit them?"

He gave a short laugh. "They don't upset her, they upset me, and for your information, Madam Psychologist, they *are* her grandparents. They over-indulge her because it's the line of least resistance. I don't put up with the same nonsense—which leads to temporary friction. It's a nuisance, but no reason to deny them access."

"No, I suppose not." Emily was hurt by the dismissive note in his voice, yet she recognized that somehow she had touched a raw nerve. She knew all about raw nerves, but she still couldn't understand why Aaron seemed to go so tough and hard whenever he was reminded of his wife's family.

"Couldn't you stay with them too when Tommy's visiting?" she asked cautiously, deciding to risk another rebuff.

"No, I couldn't."

Obviously that line would get her nowhere. "I see," she said, not seeing at all. "Um—was—I mean, did you have a problem with the grandparents even when your wife was alive?"

"My wife...?" He took a deep breath. "Emily, I don't want to discuss Tommy's mother."

She noted the small creases around his eyes, the bitter twist to his mouth, and knew she would get no more out of him this evening. Odd, she had thought the subject of Tommy's improved disposition would be a safe one. But instead Aaron had become a curt and distant stranger. Now she was beginning to wonder if there *were* any safe subjects with him. He had forced her to face her own past, it was true. But had he, in fact, faced his own?

As this thought only increased her frustration, she stood up and announced abruptly, "I hope you don't mind, but it's been a long day, and I'd like to get some sleep. Good night."

To her surprise, he only shrugged and said, "Of course. Sleep well. Thank you for your hospitality, Emily. I'll look forward to enjoying more of it tomorrow."

Emily, who was already halfway out of the door, whirled round like a mechanical top. "What?" she exclaimed. "What are you talking about, Aaron? You're leaving tomorrow."

"Am I?" One of his boots was resting on her metal magazine rack, and his smile had become altogether catlike.

"Well, yes. Your sweater will be ready in the morning..."

"Ah, but will *I* be?"

Emily grabbed the doorframe in order to forestall an urge to stamp her foot. "Of course you will!" she snapped.

"What makes you so sure?"

This time she permitted her foot a sharp tap. "I'm sure I invited you for one night. You'll have stayed two. And there is a limit to my hospitality."

He shrugged again, which only incensed her further, because she couldn't control a quiver of admiration at the way the muscles bunched against his sweatshirt. "We'll discuss it in the morning," he said, with an infuriating air of finality.

"We will *not* discuss it in the morning," retorted Emily, holding both sides of the door now for support. "In the morning you're *leaving*, Aaron Silverstone." She swung around and stalked rigidly out into the hall.

His only answer was a soft chuckle, but as she closed the door of her room she thought she heard him murmur with mocking composure, "Like hell I am, Emily Rogers! Just you wait and see!"

"The only thing *you're* going to see is the door," she muttered to herself as she slipped her nightie over her head. "I've had all I can take from you for one decade, my friend, and I'm not planning on taking any more."

But she fell asleep thinking of wet dark hair clinging to a man's tanned face. And then of a sturdy little girl who really looked quite sweet when she smiled...

Emily awoke with a headache, as well as a very bad temper and, after pulling on jeans and a shirt, hurried quietly out to the kitchen before Biscuit could start scratching down the door.

She fed an eager dog and a slightly disdainful cat who wasn't impressed with dry cat food, and was grimly mixing up eggs by the time Aaron appeared in the doorway, stretching lazily.

"What are you doing with those?" he asked with unflattering suspicion.

"Making scrambled eggs." Her reply was brief. She was in no mood for aspersions on her cooking.

"Are you sure?"

She had known he wouldn't be able to resist it. "Quite sure," she replied coldly.

"Mmm." He looked skeptical. "I hope you are, because if we're going to explore again today we'll need a hearty breakfast to start us off."

"*We* are not going to explore again today," she pointed out. "You're leaving, remember?"

"I hadn't thought of it."

"I don't care whether you'd thought of it or not." She began beating viciously at the eggs. "You've overstayed your welcome, I'm afraid."

"Such ingratitude!"

"Listen," said Emily, deserting the eggs and whirling around to face him. "Just because you rescued me from that thug the other day, it doesn't mean I owe you a lifetime of free room and board."

"No. Just a few more days' worth."

Her breath hissed out in an exasperated sigh. "Aaron, you are *not* staying a few more days!"

"Why not?" he asked, fixing her with his Grand Inquisitor look. "What are you afraid of, Emily? Me? Still?"

"No, of course not. I——"

"Then I hope you're not trying to tell me you don't like me. Because I'm not at all sure I'd believe you."

No, naturally he wouldn't believe her. He knew damn well that on those rare occasions when she wasn't plotting unpleasant ways to dispose of his mortal remains she liked him very much indeed. "It's not that," she muttered, fidgeting with a button on her shirt.

"So what is it?" He lounged across to the table and peered pensively down at the eggs.

That was easy. She wanted him to leave because she was scared out of her wits that if he stayed she might begin to care for him. And if that happened, she'd be laying herself open to hurt again. Not just because any relationship would make her vulnerable to further pain, but because Aaron was the love-'em-and-leave-'em type, as she had every reason to know. An opportunist who took advantage of any willing woman who happened to wander his way.

But she didn't want to tell him that.

"I don't know." She tried to frame an answer, moving hastily aside as his elbow brushed her bare arm. "It's—I..."

With a swiftness that shocked her out of her stuttering indecision, he seized both her elbows and spun her about to face him. "Don't waste your time searching for a plausible answer," he said roughly. "I want the truth."

"All right," said Emily, lifting her chin. "All right, Aaron. The truth is..." She hesitated, because she didn't know what the truth was.

Aaron's mouth hardened. Then suddenly, as she gaped up at him, it was pressed with brief competence to her lips.

At once, as she was sure he had known it would, her stomach seemed to melt inside her. She closed her eyes, wanting to fight him, but she couldn't. With a little moan, she surrendered herself to his kiss.

It didn't last long. Just long enough to convince her that whatever she might pretend to herself, or to him, she really didn't want him to go.

"Perhaps," he said, when he lifted his head, "that may help you to make up your mind."

Emily stared at him, wishing he didn't look so cool, so casually in command. "About what?" she demanded.

"About why you won't admit that you want me to stay."

She frowned. "I think you must be the most arrogant man I've ever met," she muttered.

"Quite possibly. Now, I propose to go for a drive. When I come back I'll expect you to be ready for another day's employment as my tourist guide."

Emily put her hands on her hips. "You can expect all you like," she told him, "but you're not my boss, Aaron Silverstone, and I *don't* have to do what you say."

"Don't you?" He smiled in a way that once again reminded Emily of a snake which was quite confident of its lunch. "I think you do."

She didn't get a chance to reply, because by the time she had framed the words Aaron had already left the room. A moment later she heard the door slam and the sound of feet crunching gravel.

"Where's Dad gone?" asked Tommy, bouncing cheerfully into the kitchen. "He looked kinda mad about something."

"Me, I expect," said Emily.

"Probably. He always gets mad at ladies. Then they don't come around any more, and I'm glad. But I wouldn't be glad about you," she added quickly.

"Wouldn't you?" Emily began to cook the eggs which Aaron had just turned his back on. If he wanted to starve, that was his problem. "Er—what did he get mad about, Tommy?" It wasn't her business, but she wanted to know.

"I dunno. Sometimes I think he didn't like them much, and he was mad at himself because he didn't."

Emily raised her eyebrows. Tommy was a very bright little girl.

The two of them consumed a companionable breakfast together. Afterward Tommy helped her clean up, then asked eagerly, "Where are we going today, Emily?"

"I don't know. Maybe just down to the beach." Emily kept her eyes on her feet, not wanting to admit even to herself that she was about to capitulate to Aaron's autocratic demands.

"Great," said Tommy. "I'll go get ready."

Emily nodded. "Yes, you do that. I guess I'll just tidy up a bit more."

But when Tommy had gone, she stared around her cluttered kitchen and decided it was as tidy as it was going to get. She was about to follow her young friend into the bedroom, when Biscuit barked, and she looked up, expecting to see Aaron.

Only the man elbowing his way through the door wasn't Aaron.

He was Andrew.

CHAPTER FIVE

EMILY stared at her visitor and groaned inwardly. Andrew was all she needed right now.

"Hi," she greeted him, without enthusiasm. "What can I do for you?"

The instant she saw the wolfish grin cross his face, she knew that had been the wrong thing to ask.

"Well, now," he said expansively, "I wouldn't want you to feel deprived, love. I see that your *overnight* visitor has departed. Perhaps I can help to fill the void."

"Andrew, stop it," said Emily, as the big man took a step toward her. "There isn't any void, and I——"

Her words were cut off as Andrew's arms swept around her in a friendly bear hug. "Come on, love," he said, "don't be a miser with your charms. You might at least give me a kiss."

"I might *not*," she said firmly, finding herself hard put to it not to laugh. Andrew was like a big, lovable animal in this mood, and he looked so woebegone when she refused him that she was almost tempted to do as he asked.

He saw her lips quirk. "Ah," he crowed, "your heart isn't made of steel after all! Just put your arms around my neck, love, that's all I ask."

Well, she could manage that if it would get him off her back. Laughing, and shaking her head at him, she lifted her arms and did as he wanted.

She didn't hear the front door open, but she did hear the sound of a step in the hall, and glanced quickly over Andrew's shoulder.

Aaron, a cynical twist distorting the firm line of his lips, was standing in the hallway watching her. When she dropped her arms like a child caught stealing candy, he turned on his heel and strode purposefully back the way he had come.

This time he didn't slam the door.

Emily stood stock-still for a moment, staring aghast at the spot where he had been. Then, dodging around Andrew, she took a quick step into the hallway. When she reached the door, she stopped. What on earth did she think she was doing? There was no reason for her to run after him. She didn't have to explain herself to Aaron. He had no hold on her, no right to criticize her actions. Slowly she swung back to Andrew, who was looking down at her with a lazy speculation she didn't trust.

"Sorry," he said, not sounding it. "I gather I've thrown a wrench in the gears."

She shook her head. "No, not really. There weren't any gears to wrench." There were, though. She wanted Aaron to leave, of course she did, but, when it came right down to it, she hated him believing that Andrew was her lover.

"Hmm," grunted the cause of her distress, quirking a thickly arched eyebrow. "I suppose you want me to go."

"Yes, please."

"And you're not going to offer me breakfast?"

"No, I'm not. We've already had it." When he continued to look at her as if he were a dog begging for crumbs, she said reluctantly, "You can come for dinner this evening if you like." She had to get rid of him somehow, and, after his one memorable encounter with her favorite soy-bean casserole, he had always turned down her invitations to dine.

"I'll think about it." He patted her on the shoulder, bent down to peck her cheek, and sauntered jauntily out into the hall. Tommy emerged from the bedroom at the same time, took one look at Emily's face, and followed him into the garden.

A few minutes later, the door snapped open again to admit Aaron. His gaze met hers with an expression that she could only interpret as contempt.

She stared at him, but when he didn't speak, against her better judgment she found herself saying, "What you saw—it wasn't..."

"There's no need to explain. Now that the situation has been clarified——"

"What situation?" she demanded, her eyes sparking sea green fire.

He shrugged. "Hatton. I didn't realise——"

"There's nothing to realize," she said, trying to keep her voice down and not succeeding. "Andrew's my neighbor, that's all."

"I see. You call that hot little scene I just witnessed being neighborly, do you? Obviously I have less accommodating neighbors. Why do you suppose that is, Emily?"

Ignoring his sarcasm with considerable effort, Emily managed not to stamp her feet, punch him on the nose, or pull his hair. She thought longingly of her childhood, when dealing with frustration had been just such a relatively simple matter...

"Listen," she said, picking up the eggbeater and pointing it at him, "it has nothing to do with you, but it just so happens that Andrew and I——"

"Are just friends?"

The taunting disbelief in his tone infuriated her, and, not for the first time around Aaron, she lost her temper.

"Right," she snapped, "that's exactly what we are. And even if we weren't, who the hell are you to talk? I've known Andrew for almost three years, and there's no reason why I shouldn't give him a friendly hug. As far as I can gather, you knew Vera for about three hours. *And* she belonged to someone else."

Aaron's eyes, which had been only coldly skeptical, registered a kind of shock. And then he frowned. "Vera?" he asked, lounging across to the table and sitting down. "Who in the blazes is Vera?"

It's a brilliant performance, thought Emily, a curious detachment replacing her spurt of temper. And she couldn't help admiring his nerve. If she hadn't known better, she could easily have believed he really had no idea what she meant.

"You're wasting your time, Aaron," she said dryly. "I stayed at that motel in Campbell River too. Vera and her husband had the room next to mine, and it had remarkably thin walls. But I suppose you were too busy to notice that little detail."

"Ah!" Again, if she hadn't been in the motel three nights ago, she would have sworn the sudden comprehension in his eyes was real. "Was her name Vera?"

"Oh, for Pete's sake," muttered Emily, disgusted. She was becoming very weary of this conversation, and, for no reason that she could put her finger on, she suddenly felt unutterably depressed. "Didn't you even bother to ask her name?"

"Why should I? She was enough damn trouble as it was, without getting personal."

"Personal! You don't call going to bed with the woman getting personal?"

"Going to... Oh, for crying out loud!" He stood up, his stance as he loomed over her almost threatening. A number of expressions crossed his face. Anger, exasperation, the desire to retaliate—but mostly just plain astonishment. "Emily," he groaned, shaking his head, "do you seriously think I wanted to make love to that drunken tart? She couldn't even stand up, for heaven's sake. I left my room to check on Tommy before turning out the light, and found the dumb dame practically passed out at my feet. She called out to me to help her to her room. I figured she was on her own, so I did."

"Naturally," said Emily, with a scornful toss of her head.

Aaron glowered at her. "What you could do with, my girl, is a damn good——"

"Yes?" she asked through her teeth, with a deliberately menacing sweetness.

He expelled his breath forcibly. "Never mind. I was contemplating a little minor violence which at this particular point in time would give me significant satisfaction. Unfortunately, apart from being inexcusably chauvinistic, which wouldn't bother me, it's probably also illegal—which would."

"How fortunate for me," jeered Emily.

"Believe me, it is."

She eyed the tight set of his mouth, and the large hands curled loosely against his thighs, and decided that perhaps she did believe him. She also began to believe that it was possible—just possible—that she'd misjudged him. As he had misjudged her.

"Do you mean you *weren't* trying to seduce Vera?" she asked, wishing he wasn't standing so close.

"That's precisely what I mean. If you'd kept your ears open, you'd have known it was the other way around. As her husband very quickly came to see. I imagine they'd both had one too many at the bar."

"Oh," said Emily, feeling limp and exceedingly foolish. When he put it like that, his version of the events in the motel made perfect sense.

"Oh? Is that all you have to say?" He put a finger beneath her chin and tilted it up, so that she couldn't evade the demanding light in his eyes.

"I'm sorry," she said woodenly. "I jumped to the wrong conclusion. So did you."

"Did I? I find it hard to disregard the evidence of my own eyes, but I suppose taller stories have proved true."

He didn't believe her. There was no particular reason why he should. "That means you're not going to apologize," she said flatly.

"That's exactly what it means. You're a bright young woman, Green Eyes. And now I think I'd better find my daughter—last seen rolling on the grass and discussing picnics with your deplorable dog."

"I made you breakfast," said Emily to his departing back. "You didn't eat it."

"Another of life's infinite blessings," he replied without turning his head.

"Aaron!" she shouted after him. "If you think..."

But Aaron wasn't listening. Her voice trailed into silence as he continued on his way to the door, opened it, and shut it very deliberately behind him.

Damn him! Emily sank down at the table and closed her eyes. If only there were some way to dent that infuriating air of superiority...

Funny, for a second there, once she'd understood about Vera, she hadn't been nearly so anxious for him to go. But of course he was still convinced that she and Andrew were an item, and it was better to leave it that way. At least now, even if he insisted on staying until tomorrow for Tommy's sake, he would eventually leave without an argument, and let her get on with her summer in peace. And she was *glad* he hadn't had any breakfast.

She stood up, pulled a brick of cheese from the fridge, and groped in a battered cardboard box for some bread. There wasn't any, which meant she'd forgotten to buy it. Oh, well, it would only take a minute to drive into town. She could pick up Aaron's sweater at the same time.

Emily was just opening the door of the Toyota when she felt a hand on her arm, and she turned around quickly, wearing an unconsciously wistful smile.

"And where do you think you're off to?" asked Aaron silkily.

"To get some food and your sweater. Do you mind?"

"Not necessarily."

"Then would you please take your hand off my elbow?"

"All in good time. First I'd like to refresh my memory."

Before she had a chance to move, he had put his hand on her waist and was pulling her none too gently into his arms.

At once she felt that curious weakness that attacked her whenever Aaron touched her. Her legs didn't seem to belong to her, and the feel of his hands on her spine was an aphrodisiac, arousing all those longings she had been so sure she wouldn't feel again. Hadn't *wanted* to feel again.

"Aaron..." she murmured, her lips on the cool skin of his throat, and her fingers, which she couldn't seem to control, clutching at the collar of his shirt. "Aaron..."

Then his mouth closed over hers, cutting off all further thought or speech.

Cutting off her breath too, she became vaguely aware, after moments that seemed endless had passed. There was a sweet warmth pulsing through her veins, a warmth she wanted to hold on to forever. But she couldn't breathe, her lungs were bursting...and Aaron was holding her away.

"Mmm," he said, "that's what I thought. You taste of rose petals and burnt scrambled egg. Unusual, but I could get used to it."

"Oh," gasped Emily. "Oh! How dare you? How could you?"

"It wasn't difficult," he said softly. "And now I can be sure you won't forget me."

She turned away, fumbled with the handle of the car. Forget him, she thought furiously, as she stumbled on to the seat. *Forget* him. Who could possibly forget a jerk like him? And what was he talking about now? She was only going into town for food. Come to think of it, even if she'd been off on a flying visit to Mars, there wasn't much chance she would ever completely forget Aaron—who was watching her drive off with his hands resting on his hips and a cool smile flicking the corner of his mouth.

When she arrived home three-quarters of an hour later, though, and discovered that Aaron and Tommy had vanished, it occurred to Emily that he might very well have decided to forget her.

There was no sign of the station wagon in the clearing, and Buster and Biscuit were alone in the kitchen looking reproachful. She opened the door for them and wandered into the bedroom. There was a sweater of Tommy's in the closet, but no sign of her jacket. She looked in the living room. Aaron's belongings were gone too, but that didn't mean much because he'd kept most of them in the car so as not to clutter up her small house.

She frowned. Had he and Tommy gone? Without saying goodbye? Surely even *he* wouldn't—oh. That kiss. And Aaron saying that now he could be sure she wouldn't forget him. He had been angry about Andrew, even if he hadn't exactly said so. Was this his revenge?

A horn hooted somewhere down the lane, and she glanced quickly out of the window. But it wasn't Aaron.

Another half hour passed, and Emily checked the cupboards again and discovered a pair of Aaron's shoes. But he usually wore boots, so perhaps he'd decided to leave these...

By quarter to twelve she'd given up. Aaron wasn't coming back. He had gone for good, leaving the field clear for Andrew.

Feeling as if her heart had turned unexpectedly to lead, Emily picked up the phone to call Yvonne.

Yvonne, who was a kindhearted friend, listened patiently. "Yes," she agreed, when Emily had finished, "I guess he has gone. Do you mind?"

"No," said Emily, who minded very much. "Why should I?"

"Because you've just spent ten minutes telling me what an arrogant bastard he is—when he's not being a wonderful cook."

"Well, that's hardly a recommendation," protested Emily.

"Not for a husband, I agree, but it might do very well for a nice bit of misbehavior in the hay."

"Yvonne! I don't do that sort of thing, and you know it. Besides, I don't have any hay."

"So get some. If you don't watch out, you'll turn into a dried-up old prune, Emily Rogers. Then you'll be sorry." Emily could almost see the pert little blonde tossing her head.

She laughed without much conviction. "No, I won't—be sorry, I mean. Listen, Yvonne..."

"Uh-huh?"

"Would you do me a favor?"

"Depends what it is."

"It's Andrew. You know he's been pestering me for years—with flowers, invitations, outrageous flattery, and, when all else has failed, downright bullying?"

"Yes," agreed Yvonne dryly, "you have mentioned it a hundred or so times."

"And now that he's got this idea about Aaron and me I just know he's going to get worse. I suppose you wouldn't like to take him off my hands, would you?"

Yvonne giggled. "Your generosity overwhelms me. I don't know, Em..."

"He likes blondes," said Emily hopefully. "You like the artistic type, don't you? And you've just broken off with—what was his name?"

"Conor. And just because he only lasted a week it doesn't mean you needn't remember his name." Yvonne sucked in her breath. "Are you trying to say you want me to exercise my wiles on the man? Trap him into a flaming affair just to draw the heat off you?"

"Yes," admitted Emily guiltily, "I guess I am."

Yvonne laughed, not in the least offended. "All right—why not? I've met your Andrew, and I rather fancied him, but he was taken up with that redheaded model at the time. I'll have a go at him."

"Thanks, friend," said Emily with a sigh of gratitude. "I owe you one."

"Oh, you'll pay, never fear."

But Emily knew she wouldn't. Yvonne was too generous hearted.

She sighed again as she put down the phone and stared around the empty house. She had always enjoyed its peace and solitude, but just now it seemed much too quiet, especially without Tommy's laughter. If it became too quiet, she could even envisage a time when she might miss Aaron's autocratic baritone demanding instant attention.

Biscuit scratched on the door. Emily opened it, and immediately wished she hadn't, as any lingering regret for Aaron's company was vanquished by the need for prompt action.

"Oh!" she cried. "Biscuit, you horrible hound! What *have* you been rolling in this time?"

Biscuit panted up at her happily and wagged his tail.

Emily headed for her small bathroom and turned on the tap.

A short time later, a thoroughly disgruntled dog was in the bath. Emily, dripping with dirty water and dog hair, was struggling to keep him there. She knew that if she didn't remove the unmentionable splodge he had been rolling in with canine abandon, he would eventually succeed in spreading it all over the house.

She had just made a successful lunge at the culprit's neck, and was half lying in the bath with her posterior draped over the rim, when a voice that she hadn't expected to hear again, and didn't much want to hear at this moment, drawled just behind her, "Tempting—very tempting. A little damp perhaps, and a little dirty, but none the less appealing for that."

As Emily's body twitched in shock, the voice added carelessly, "In case you wondered, I wasn't referring to the dog."

CHAPTER SIX

EMILY choked, lost her grip on Biscuit, grabbed for him, and ended up face down in the water with her legs sprawled over the edge.

She didn't hear the man behind her exclaim, "Oh, for crying out loud!" Nor did she hear the more expressive epithet that followed, because she was too busy trying to wriggle her way out of a situation which was as uncomfortable as it was undignified. In fact, she couldn't ever remember feeling this embarrassed in her life. But as she kicked her feet helplessly, she most certainly did feel the hand on the neck of her shirt, and the fingers sliding efficiently under the waistband of her saturated khaki shorts.

In the next instant she was jerked upward, and then she was half lying, half standing with her back against a man's broad chest. She could still feel his fingers where they had no business, and involuntarily she gave a little shiver.

"Cold?" Aaron's voice murmured in her ear.

"No. I——"

She got no further, because at that point Biscuit, who up until now had been stunned into immobility by his mistress's unheard-of intrusion into his bath, took advantage of the lull to leap for freedom. In the space of half a second he was out of the bath. In another second he had shaken a deluge of droplets all over the floor, walls and ceiling, and immediately after that he was bounding eagerly through the open door to wreak further havoc in the kitchen.

"Biscuit!" wailed Emily. "Oh, Lord, he'll turn the whole house into a puddle! Aaron, let me go..."

But Aaron had already released her, and was pounding in pursuit of the excited dog, who was now happily spreading chaos in the hall.

By the time Emily had regained her breath and caught up with him, Biscuit was already outside playing with Tommy. She could hear the girl's delighted laughter rippling through the open window. Aaron, with his arms folded on his chest, was leaning against a firmly closed front door looking tiresomely cool and unruffled in boots, tight jeans and a blue shirt.

"What are you doing here?" gasped Emily, turning a dull red as she confronted the source of her discomfiture. "I thought you'd gone—for good."

"Sorry to disappoint you. I did consider leaving, as a matter of fact. Now I'm rather glad I didn't." He ran his eyes over her dripping wet body with a suggestive appreciation that made her head spin. It also made her want to slap his face.

"Incidentally, I thought you told me you always lock your door," he went on. There was a definite note of censure in his voice.

"Not this time," snapped Emily, furiously conscious of the spectacle she was making of herself, and of the fact that she couldn't stop blushing. "Biscuit rolled in something disgusting, and as soon as I smelled him I threw him—well, dragged him—into the bath."

"Really? It looked the other way around to me."

Emily glared at him, but he only smiled and asked impassively, "Did you manage to finish the job?"

Her shoulders sagged. "I don't know, but I sure hope so, because I don't think I could stand to start again."

She looked so woebegone that Aaron's features softened. "Come on," he said, taking a purposeful step forward, "let's get you cleaned up."

Emily jumped hastily backward as she saw that he was about to unbutton her wet shirt. "I can manage, thanks," she gulped. "I—I'll get changed. What about Tommy? Doesn't she want to come in?"

"Not in the least. I fear Biscuit has supplanted both of us in her affections."

Emily nodded. "Very natural," she agreed vaguely. "Um—yes, all right, I'll go and get changed."

"I like you wet," observed Aaron, pushing a lock of damp hair behind her ear.

Emily didn't doubt it, so she backed away even faster and slammed the bedroom door in his face.

She leaned against it, gasping, oblivious now to the clinging wetness of her grubby shirt and shorts. Up until this moment, there had been so much going on that she hadn't had time to sort out how she felt about the fact that Aaron hadn't left after all. Surprised, certainly. Confused, terribly. Afraid? Yes, that too. But underneath the surprise and the confusion and nervousness, as well as the inevitable irritation, she had to admit there was also a little warm glow of pleasure—a sense that her life was about to begin again in an area that was totally unexpected.

She shook a strand of fiery wet hair out of her eyes, reminding herself that this was all fruitless speculation. What she had to do now was change into something that would be attractive, without inviting that look of contemplative lechery in Aaron's eye.

Then, perhaps, they would talk.

She peeled off the offending clothes, dressed quickly in a clean white blouse and a denim skirt, and went to look for him.

She found him stretched out on the sofa in her living room looking for all the world as if he owned it. His face was invisible behind a copy of yesterday's paper.

"I've changed," said Emily in a small voice. "Now what?"

He allowed the paper to drop slowly onto the floor, and grinned irritatingly. "I'm not sure. This is the first time a woman has attempted to drown herself the moment I spoke to her. I can't decide if I find it flattering or not."

Emily smiled. It was a doubtful sort of smile, because the sight of him spread over her sofa with his legs a little apart, his shirt unbuttoned and his lips curved in that memorable grin, was doing very disturbing things to her libido.

"Don't worry, I wasn't attempting suicide," she assured him. "I just didn't expect a man to wander into my bathroom and start making remarks about my..." She stopped abruptly, realizing too late what she was saying.

"Your delightful bottom," he finished for her, glancing approvingly at the part of her under discussion. "Why not? It's precisely the sort of bottom I like to remark on."

Emily sighed. This was getting them nowhere. "What I mean is, what are you doing here? Or hadn't you actually left? And is Tommy still expecting a picnic?"

"'Course I am," said an aggrieved voice from outside the open window. "But Dad said we had to go for a long drive first, and then all he did was stop for breakfast. I'd already *had* my breakfast."

Aaron looked at his daughter and murmured something that sounded like "deepest sympathies."

Emily glowered. "I don't see why you won't trust my cooking," she snapped. "I do try—sometimes."

"I know you do. That's just the trouble. But since you brought it up, is there some reason why I *ought* to trust your cooking? Have circumstances changed in the short time since last we met?" He glanced pointedly at his watch.

No, circumstances hadn't changed at all. She still wanted to kick him. But his eyes were gleaming at her and his mouth was curved in a caustically crooked grin that somehow turned her resolutions to water.

So she laughed instead. There didn't seem much else to do.

"By the way," said Aaron with lazy complacence, "although I caught up with your Hound of the Baskervilles as fast as I could, I believe there is still some evidence of his passage in the hall."

"Yes, and in the bathroom," sighed Emily. "Back in a minute."

By the time she had removed Aaron's "evidence" from the bath, walls, light fixtures and hall rug—which Biscuit had apparently used as a towel—it was well into the afternoon, and Tommy was jumping impatiently about on one foot.

"When are we *going*?" she demanded.

"When we're ready," said Aaron.

"Right away," said Emily.

"I like Emily's answer better," said Tommy.

"Surprise, surprise," muttered Aaron.

Fifteen minutes later, after Emily had thrown any food that wasn't actually moving into the cooler, the three of them climbed into the station wagon to drive to the beach.

It was a warm, sleepy sort of day with the sun beating down on the sand and a faint haze misting over the islands. When Tommy and Aaron went to swim, Emily, in her black bathing suit, lay back on the blanket and announced that she'd had quite enough water for one day, thank you, and was proposing to rest for a while.

She had no idea how much time had passed when she awoke from a light sleep to feel something warm touch her skin. She opened her eyes to find Aaron leaning over her with an elbow propped on the blanket while he dribbled a trail of sand deliberately up and down her chest.

She sat up quickly.

"Aaron—" she began warningly.

"It's all right. Tommy's over there—in sight and out of earshot. And I wasn't planning to steal your virtue on a busy beach."

"It's already been stolen," said Emily. "Six years ago. Which doesn't mean you're having the seconds."

"Not at the moment, I agree." He turned his head away briefly, and she was almost sure he was hiding a smile.

"Did you really mean to go away this morning?" she asked, moving to the edge of the blanket as he reached to put his arm around her waist.

"I considered it briefly, when I saw you laughing in the arms of your rather dissolute-looking neighbor. Especially as I recalled that you'd been attempting to speed me on my way more or less from the moment I crossed your threshold. Brawling over a woman is hardly my style."

"No, I suppose all you have to do is open your arms and they come tumbling into them. I must be an unpleasant shock."

"Oh, you're not a shock. You *have* tumbled, after all. Although you can certainly make yourself unpleasant when you want to. That's something I'll have to deal with in short order." He shifted his body smoothly across the blanket and curved his fingers around the back of her neck.

"Take your hand off me," said Emily coldly. "Brawling may not be your style, but mauling obviously is."

"Don't you like it?" he asked, moving his thumb tantalizingly over the skin just below her left ear.

She did like it—very much. And he knew it. "Aaron," she said, taking a deep, controlling breath, "why won't you go and leave me in peace?"

"I told you, I thought about it and decided against it. When I put my mind to it, I usually get what I want. And in this case I'm not impressed by the competition."

Emily caught his hand and pushed it away. "I'm not a juicy bone for you to compete over like a couple of dogs," she complained, unable to disguise her exasperation. "But if you mean Andrew, I told you, he *is* just a neighbor. Why in the world won't you believe me?"

"Oh, I always did believe you after a fashion," Aaron said lightly. "Or at least conceded that you might be telling me the truth."

"Then why...?"

He gave a twisted smile. "On the other hand, you've been *very* insistent that I should leave. There has to be a reason."

"Well, it's not Andrew," she replied irritably. "As a matter of fact, I've just set him up with my friend

Yvonne.'' She glanced away because his eyes were smoldering at her and demanding an explanation at the same time, and she felt a terrible urge to put her arms around him.

Tommy came running toward them along the sand, and Emily heaved a sigh of relief. Nothing had been settled. Aaron was presumably staying another night. But at least for the moment she was safe from the persuasive magnetism of his eyes and his hands and—she shivered—and everything that went to make up this devastating, disturbing, totally infuriating man.

Later the three of them had dinner at the Inn on the Beach, and Tommy entertained them with tales of her friend Margaret, who had something she called a ''Vetnameze'' pot-bellied pig. Aaron didn't say much, for which Emily was thankful.

Again, Tommy was tired when they got home and didn't stay up very long. After she had gone to bed Emily made coffee and carried it into the living room, wondering how she could bring up the subject of Aaron's departure—and also wondering if she wanted to bring it up at all.

He was lying on the sofa again, watching her thoughtfully as she sat down, crossed her legs, and pushed her hair unnecessarily behind her ears. It wasn't the speculative, predatory watching that had unnerved her so often in the past, but rather a sort of warm, possessive look, as if they had sat like this many times before, and would again. As if Aaron actually belonged there on her sofa, smiling lazily, and making her want to smile back.

The thought startled her, and she wasn't sure she liked it. She didn't want to smile either. She wanted to know what was happening to her.

"Aaron," she said quietly, "this is my house, you know. You can't just move in and settle down."

"Can't I? And what about Tommy?"

"Tommy? What's she got to do with it?"

"Quite a lot. She likes it here."

"Well, yes, that's all very well, but—anyway, she assures me she always has to do what *you* want to do on your holidays."

"She exaggerates. But as it happens, I have a reason for wanting her to stay here at the moment." He had been lying back with his hands loosely clasped behind his head, but now he sat up and leaned forward. "The point is, my daughter has recently enjoyed a particularly satisfactory visit with her grandparents, during which she was overfed and thoroughly spoiled. This was followed, inevitably, by the usual clamping down when she got home. I've had problems with staff at work lately which, I have to admit, hasn't improved my temper." He shrugged and ran a hand through his hair. "As a result, I've been inclined to bellow a lot instead of just telling her to smarten up, and making it stick. The fact is, Emily, you have an improving effect on Tommy's disposition."

Emily heard a weary sincerity behind the lightly spoken words, and she frowned, not altogether understanding.

"Why?" she asked baldly. "Aaron, if these visits to her grandparents cause so much trouble, why don't you talk to them, make them see what they're doing...?" Vaguely, she was conscious that they had had a similar conversation once before, but his answer this time puzzled her.

"I have," he said shortly. "They don't agree. And I don't choose to talk to them again. As I told you before, it's more of an annoyance than anything. They're good to her."

"I still don't see," said Emily slowly. "You're her father. Surely you have certain legal rights..."

"Possibly. Possibly I have none whatever. And I don't intend to find out." When he saw her open her mouth to object, he stood up suddenly and strode across to the window. "Don't ask any more questions, Emily." His voice was curt, rasping. "Because I won't answer them. Just be kind to Tommy, that's all I ask."

"Of course I'll be kind to Tommy," said Emily indignantly. "But I'm not a psychologist, Aaron."

"I don't want a psychologist," he snapped. "I just want you to mind your own business."

She gasped, feeling her face suffuse with color. She didn't know what had caused this startling change of mood, but she knew she didn't have to take it.

She jumped up to confront him, snagging her watch on a loose thread trailing from a cushion. Wrenching it free, she flung the cushion back on the chair, and took a quick step toward him.

"Aaron," she said to his rigid back, "you have no right to walk into my house expecting to make yourself at home here, and then start ordering me to mind my own business." She spoke in the sort of voice she normally reserved for the impudent teenagers who sometimes disrupted her class. "I love your daughter, of course I do, but I'm damned if I'm going to be treated like your servant. No, *worse* than that, because no servant today would put up with your sort of arrogance. And I'm not putting up with it either. You can stay tonight for Tommy's sake, but tomorrow, first thing, you're leaving——"

"No, I'm not," said Aaron, swinging around, and speaking so calmly that she stopped in mid-tirade.

She had been so busy unloading her hurt and indignation, and hitting back at Aaron for his inexcusable rudeness, that she hadn't noticed the gradual change in his expression. His face was no longer bleak and uncompromising, and the eyes that had been smoldering like black ice now showed only surprise and, if she was not much mistaken, approval.

"You're beautiful when you're angry," he said softly, his mouth curving in amused admiration.

He meant it. He actually meant it, Emily thought, barely able to credit this stunning about-face. What was more, he had just used one of the oldest lines in the world, and managed to make it sound as though he were the first man who had ever employed it.

"Is that bit of overused flattery supposed to make me roll around at your feet like Biscuit?" she asked dryly.

Aaron cocked an eyebrow and looked pensive. "It would be nice," he admitted. "Are you going to?"

Oh, hell, she thought. If he goes on looking at me like that, I just might. What *is* it about him that can turn me into a spineless amoeba with no more than a hint of his smile?

"No," she said hastily, "I'm not."

"I was afraid you weren't. Ah, well, there are alternatives."

Before she could take in what he was doing, he had closed the gap between them, seized her around the hips and dragged her down with him onto the pale green carpet. There was a small stain beside the coffee table that she hadn't noticed before. It was just on the edge of her vision when she jerked her face away so she wouldn't have to look into his eyes.

"There," he said complacently. "Now nobody's at anybody's feet. But there's nothing to stop us rolling, which in the long run may prove a much more satisfactory arrangement."

"Oh!" cried Emily, as his arm trapped her against him. "Aaron, stop it! What do you think you're doing?" She began to squirm furiously against the hard angles of his body, but his only reaction to that was to laugh softly and hold her closer.

"Keep that up," he murmured, "and I won't be thinking at all—I'll be doing."

That quietened her, because she didn't have to ask *what* he would be doing. She could feel his reaction with no difficulty at all through the tight fabric of his dark blue jeans. And as she drew in her breath she had no choice but to accept that her own desire was as great, or greater, than his. Quite suddenly, all doubt and all resistance crumbled and she knew that in this moment all she wanted in the world was Aaron. Wanted with an urgency and a hungry craving that made everything else seem meaningless and unimportant.

But the feeling only lasted a few seconds.

As Aaron's hand slipped beneath her skirt, a movement in the corner of the room caught her eye. A white movement. Buster. Buster, who was beloved of Tommy. Tommy, who was asleep in the bedroom...

"Don't, Aaron," she moaned. "Please don't. I can't... Tommy."

He removed his hand at once. "Don't worry, she never wakes up," he whispered into her hair. Then he sighed heavily. "But you're right, of course, this is no way to repay your hospitality. I meant to show you that sarcasm would get you nowhere, Emily, but it very nearly got both of us much further than I intended. Come on, get up!" He gave her a smart pat on the backside, eased himself onto his feet and held out a hand to help her up.

She took it, and he pulled her up beside him. For a while she just stood there, dazed and unbelieving.

"I'm sorry," he said gruffly, smoothing a hand down her cheek.

"Sorry?" She stared at him, eyes glazed.

"Oh, not for that stimulating interlude on the floor. I'm damned if I'll apologize for that, even though my instincts did get the better of my manners. But I shouldn't have told you to mind your own business." The faint lines close to his eyes seemed to deepen. "I'm afraid I'm not much good at keeping my temper where Tommy and her family are concerned."

"No," she said, gazing down at the large hand covering hers, "I've noticed you're not." Then she gave herself a quick mental shake and pulled away. "We'll forget about your instincts," she said firmly. "And as for manners, I doubt if you had many of those to forget. As to your temper..." She shook her head, still trying to bring the room back into focus. "As to your temper—well, I guess I should be grateful you have one, in a way. It came in useful the other day, didn't it?" This last thought occurred to her with some surprise.

"Did it?" He looked startled and a little annoyed.

"When you slugged that thug."

"Oh, I see. So my temper rates higher than my manners."

There was a repressive note in his voice, and she wondered for a moment if she'd gone too far. Then she remembered that *he* was the one who had gone too far, so she tossed her head and said he'd definitely got that right.

"I suggest you watch your tongue, my girl," he replied without emphasis, but in a way that made her wonder if he meant it. "If you don't, you may find out about my temper." His eyes traveled over her disheveled hair and the blouse hanging out of her skirt. "By the way, did I hear you saying something on the phone about them catching that candidate for a facial rearrangement?"

Emily, who had been about to express her candid opinion on the subject of overbearing travel consultants, chuckled instead. She was thankful that this scene appeared to be shifting from high drama to a less highly charged arena. "Yes, you did. I forgot to tell you. He was picked up for a series of assaults along the highway just this morning, and is now safely tucked away behind bars."

"For a long time, I hope."

"In theory. In practice, probably not."

"Hmm. Just as long as he doesn't try to get at you again."

Emily's eyes narrowed. Aaron was facing her with his legs apart and his jaw thrust out aggressively, looking for all the world like a stallion spoiling for a fight over his mate. Which she wasn't. But it was an interesting concept.

"He won't come near me again," she said lightly. "And now, if you don't mind, I think I've had enough excitement for one evening. I'm going to bed."

She waited for the inevitable suggestive offer but, to her surprise, it didn't come. Aaron only smiled in a pensive sort of way and said, "Good night, then. Sleep well."

In the morning Emily was awakened early by the crows. She could see them perched in the tall fir trees through a chink in her virginal white curtains. She stared at them, thinking that their cacophany somewhat echoed the confusion in her mind.

At one stage last night she had told Aaron he would have to leave first thing. But the force of that ultimatum seemed to have dissipated later, lost somewhere during that improbable scuffle on the floor. Also there was Tommy to consider. She didn't want to hurt Tommy, who from the sounds of it needed her friendship. And that was another thing. She didn't understand how Aaron...

But then when had she ever understood Aaron? That was the problem. He never mentioned his marriage, seemed to dislike his dead wife, and, although he displayed a certain tolerance for his in-laws, he obviously didn't care for them either...

In the end, any decision about the length of her guests' visit was taken out of her hands by Tommy's optimistic litany of all the things she still wanted to do in Cinnamon Bay. It was a list that would take at least another month to cover, and Emily hadn't the heart or the inclination to rain on Tommy's parade by telling her she couldn't stay.

For the next few days, to her enormous relief, everything went smoothly. The weather cooperated, they were able to go swimming and picnicking, and as Tommy was almost constantly with them, in company with numerous new friends, there was no chance of a replay of that unfortunate nonevent on the pale green carpet.

But at the end of the week, one evening when Tommy had gone to bed unusually early, Aaron stopped Emily as she was about to carry their coffee into the living room.

"Hold it," he said. "It's time you and I stopped spending our evenings like an old married couple with the essential ingredient missing."

"I don't see why," said Emily, who was under no illusions as to which ingredient he meant. "It suits me perfectly. I get an excellent cook with only minor inconvenience, you get——"

"I, Green Eyes, will eventually get you," he said softly. "And you'll find I can be very inconvenient."

"You don't have to convince me," said Emily, dodging sideways as he reached for her arm, and picking up the cups so he couldn't stop her without causing an accident. "We'll drink this in the living room as usual," she added firmly. "Biscuit, Buster, come along."

Somewhat to her surprise, both animals trotted obediently in her wake.

"Good grief," muttered Aaron as he followed them, "a bloody bodyguard! You don't think they'll do you any good, do you?"

"Yes," said Emily airily, "as a matter of fact I do."

She was right. Buster immediately moved in to sit on Aaron, digging his claws into his victim's jeans with an expression of sybaritic bliss. Aaron's expression was not blissful as he scowled down at the contented cat. It was positively malevolent. Nor did his disposition appear to improve much when Biscuit padded over to offer him a succession of demanding paws.

"Good Lord," he muttered, "you meant it! A four-legged Praetorian guard."

"Does that make me an empress?" asked Emily, smiling innocently.

"That's not the title I had in mind," he growled.

"Hmm." She eyed him warily, but, as he was making no attempt to remove Buster or eject Biscuit, she decided she wouldn't ask him to elaborate. Besides, it was fairly evident that any title he might be inclined to bestow on her at this moment would not be of the complimentary kind.

Biscuit offered another paw, and Buster purred warmly.

By the time Emily retired to bed that night, her eyes were smarting and her insides hurting from the effort to control her laughter. Aaron barely managed to snap, "Good night."

The following evening, when her pets were again recruited for guard duty, Aaron endured it for about fifteen minutes, and then said in a very tight voice, "Emily, is there some reason why you can't keep these hairy conversation stoppers in the kitchen? There's nothing worth eating in there anyway."

For once Emily, who knew full well that lack of conversation had nothing to do with his irritability, didn't rise to this blatant provocation. "No, I can't," she replied with smiling inflexibility. "This is their home too, if you don't mind, and I happen to like them in here."

Aaron rolled his eyes at the ceiling, scratched Buster's neck, accepted another paw from Biscuit and said nothing.

Emily smiled smugly, but her satisfaction lessened somewhat when she happened to glance up from a TV program on eliminating house pests of the six-legged variety to find Aaron's gaze fixed on her with narrow-eyed resolution. She didn't trust that look. She'd seen it before when he was planning to get his own way.

Which was why she was surprised when another two days passed without his making any further effort to cross the invisible barrier she had erected. Gradually she began to relax. As long as she was able to keep him at a physical distance, Aaron was an amusing and only vaguely threatening companion—and, as far as she was concerned, there was no reason why this happy state of affairs should not continue.

On the third day Andrew and Yvonne came over while Aaron was at the beach with Tommy. Emily's matchmaking had evidently proved more than successful.

"We're off for a sexy two weeks in Yellowknife," announced Yvonne breezily. "Not that I ever thought of Yellowknife as the sort of place one goes on sexy getaways, but Andrew says it is, and, anyway, he has an exhibition there."

"Have a wonderful time," laughed Emily, who was privately of the opinion that Andrew would say sex was where you made it, and that an ice floe would do nicely in a pinch.

Andrew grinned. "See what you're missing, Emily, love," he teased her. But she could see the caressing look in his eyes as he put his arm around Yvonne, and they both knew he didn't mean it.

"What was that creep doing here?" asked Aaron, arriving back a few minutes after they left. "I saw him get in a car with the dippy blonde."

"Andrew is not a creep. And Yvonne is my best friend," said Emily frostily. "They're going to Yellowknife together."

"Good place for them," muttered Aaron.

Emily contemplated placing a size seven foot on his backside as he lounged away from her, but she decided he might take that as encouragement, and reluctantly gave up the idea. Aaron had a habit of going all taciturn and glowering whenever Andrew turned up. All the same, she knew she would have missed Yvonne's company if

Aaron and Tommy had not been around to keep her busy.

She continued to appreciate their company for several more days. Then one afternoon Tommy arrived back from a brief shopping expedition to announce eagerly that Caroline Oliphant's mother had asked her to go to Vancouver with them for a week.

"Oliphant?" said Aaron. "That black-haired sprite you've been swimming with? Tommy, I don't know her mother. It's out of the question."

Tommy's face crumpled into something that resembled a resentful potato. "But, Dad," she protested as two large tears filled what could be seen of her eyes, "Dad, that's not fair——"

"Life rarely is," snapped Aaron.

Emily glanced at him. She could see that he wasn't enjoying his role as the heavy father, but he obviously hadn't a clue how to soften the blow. From his point of view it would be irresponsible—and probably insane—to let his eleven-year-old daughter go off for a week with a stranger. And that was the end of the matter.

"Aaron," said Emily carefully, "I've known the Oliphants ever since I moved here. And the family's lived in Cinnamon Bay for fifty years. They practically built it. I've had all the children in my class at one time or another, and, honestly, they're a charming family——"

"Dr. Jekyll was charming," growled Aaron.

"No, I mean they're responsible. Tommy would be well looked after."

"Please, Dad," pleaded Tommy, looking more like a little brown bird now than a potato, as her eyes flashed anxiously from one adult to the other.

"All right, I'll talk to Mrs. Oliphant," said Aaron, giving Emily a quelling look.

It was only after he had indeed talked to Caroline's mother, and the matter had been settled to Tommy's satisfaction, that it dawned on Emily what she'd done.

"You'll have to stay at the Inn till Tommy gets back," she said breathlessly to Aaron when they returned to the cottage after waving an excited Tommy and five Oliphants on their way. "You can't possibly stay here alone with just me."

"Why not?" asked Aaron. They were standing on the front step, and Emily had her hands pressed defensively back against the door. "I have every intention of staying here with just you. In fact, I've been counting on it."

He put one hand on her shoulder and spun her around, and, with the other, removed the key from her peculiarly nerveless fingers and turned the lock.

The door opened, he pushed her gently but deliberately inside, and closed it with a definitive click.

CHAPTER SEVEN

"BISCUIT!" cried Emily with overplayed affection, as the big dog bounded into the hall and leaped up to plant a wet kiss on her nose. "*There* you are. Good dog. *Very* good dog." She pulled away from Aaron and dropped to the floor to give her furry companion a fervent and ostentatious hug.

"Saved by the welcoming committee," muttered Aaron, as Buster, tail erect, joined Biscuit at Emily's knee.

"What?" Emily glanced up at him, flushed and puzzled.

"The Praetorian guard," he said, gesturing at the two pets.

"Guard?" she repeated blankly.

"Protection against the Big Bad Wolf—namely me. That's what you're thinking, isn't it?"

She swallowed. "No, of course not..."

"Good. Because I'm about to put them outside. You and I have a bit of business to finish."

"No, we haven't. And they don't want to go outside."

"Yes, they do. Look, Buster's already at the door."

"Traitor," groaned Emily beneath her breath.

"What did you say?"

"Nothing," she mumbled, scrambling to her feet because there was no longer any excuse for groveling on the floor, and, anyway, she felt less vulnerable standing up.

Aaron released the two animals on to the plot of uncultivated fenced woodland behind the cottage. Then he strolled back into the hall, folded his arms, and leaned his shoulders against the doorjamb.

"Well?" he said, eyes narrowing quizzically. "What shall we do first?"

"Eat?" suggested Emily, in a high, unnatural voice that made him smile.

He looked at his watch. "It's only three o'clock. I hope you're not trying to gain weight, Green Eyes, because I like you just the way you are. Besides, to the best of my recollection, there's nothing that resembles food in your kitchen."

Emily relaxed, less apprehensive now that he was back on that old familiar ground. "If you don't like my lifestyle you can leave," she said, trying not to sound too hopeful.

"Not on your life! With the right sort of encouragement, I've no doubt your housekeeping skills will improve. Rapidly."

It didn't take much imagination to figure out what sort of encouragement he meant, so Emily decided not to press the matter. She fixed him with what she hoped was a quelling stare. "Aaron, what do you expect to gain from staying here alone with me?" she demanded. "Everyone in Cinnamon Bay will think——"

"To answer your first point, I would have thought that was obvious. And everyone in Cinnamon Bay can think what they like."

The pale green of her eyes turned to emerald. "Don't you ever give up?"

"No. Not when I mean to win."

Emily turned her back on him and stamped off into the kitchen. "You're as bad as Andrew!" she threw at him over her shoulder.

"No, I'm not. I've no idea what your experience with Andrew is, but I promise you I'll be a whole lot better."

She could feel his breath on her neck, and she swung around indignantly, her hand raised to land a sharp slap on his cheek.

But he caught it and pulled her toward him, his other arm going smartly around her waist.

"Don't try it," he warned. "Two can play at that game."

"You wouldn't!"

"I might—I've been sorely tempted on occasion. But I'd much rather kiss you."

The look in his eyes was a dark, smoky velvet, and Emily longed to be drawn into their hypnotic depths. But she knew that if she gave in now she would be lost. Perhaps forever. And if she allowed that to happen, then her feelings would be exposed again, open to all the hurt and guilt she had worked so hard to put behind her. Oh, it would be easy, too easy, to fall in love with Aaron, who wanted only a summer affair. And even if it turned out he wanted more, it could make no difference. Because she knew all too well what love led to. It led to pain, regret, another's life inextricably entwined with one's own. And if something happened to that other life, then all that was left was heartache.

She took one last look at his eyes, soft now and seductive. Then she drew a quick breath and turned away.

Aaron sighed. "All right. I'm a patient man," he said, in that sexy voice that sent tremors up her spine. And, without further protest, he let her go.

Emily glanced back at him doubtfully. Patient? That wasn't how she would have described him, but perhaps when he wanted something enough...

The thought trailed off, leaving her more disturbed than before.

After that she made tea. Then she fed Buster and Biscuit, started to rummage in the fridge for supper, and fed a delighted Buster and Biscuit all over again.

Aaron had been sitting at the kitchen table watching her, not saying much, but when he saw her provide the animals with a second meal, he asked in a voice that wasn't as steady as usual, "Something on your mind, Emily? Or do you always supply hot and cold running pet food?"

Emily gaped at the dishes which were now being rapidly emptied, and ran a hand across her forehead. Then she shook her head, gulped, and burst out laughing.

"No," she choked, "not usually. What's more, this is all your fault."

"I thought it might be," he replied, sounding more smug than repentant.

Emily shook her head again and gave up. But after that the strain that had hung in the air between them seemed to dissolve, and they were able to eat supper—a lentil concoction which Aaron ploughed through with martyred resignation—in an atmosphere of wary amiability.

They spent the evening leafing through the papers and watching summer repeats on TV. Around eleven o'clock, when Emily yawned and murmured something about needing her sleep, Aaron looked up from an article on climbing in the Rockies, and smiled at her. It was a bland, friendly smile, and she didn't trust it an inch. She met his eyes boldly, sure that he would take the opportunity to resume his efforts to insinuate his way into her bedroom.

But he didn't. He merely said, "Good night, Green Eyes," and went on reading his article.

Contrarily, Emily felt a stab of something which she was horrified to realize was disappointment.

Ten minutes later she pulled on her sleeveless white nightshirt with the picture of Mickey Mouse on it, heaped up the pillows and settled back in bed to read her book. It was a large tome entitled *Healthy Eating*. She had bought it in a moment of misguided nutritional fever, and had since discovered that it was almost guaranteed to induce healthy sleep.

But tonight it didn't work. Her eye fixed on the words, "irritability, anxiety, light-headedness, dizziness, insomnia and fatigue."

That's me, she thought disgustedly, reading on to discover the cause of all these afflictions, and not unduly surprised to find that it wasn't Aaron Silverstone, but sugar.

Just then she heard Aaron emerge from the bathroom. He paused outside her door. "Good night," he said softly. "Don't wait up for me."

Don't wait...! Emily opened her mouth to give him a piece of her mind, and found herself smiling instead.

"Good night," she replied. And then, as she heard him move away, "Aaron?"

"Mmm?"

What had she wanted to say? Her confused gaze fell on the book, grasped mindlessly at a word. "Aaron—what's black cohosh?"

He gave a strangled exclamation, hit his foot on the telephone table, and stepped back. "Do you really want to know?"

"Yes, of course." What else could she say?

The door opened slowly, and he stuck his head in. "It's a rare medicinal herb found in Pennsylvania. Maybe other places."

Emily blinked. "How did you know that?"

"You gather a lot of useless information in the travel business—at least I do. What on earth are you reading?"

She held up the book, and, without saying a word, or making it seem anything but natural, he walked into the room and took it from her.

"Healthy Eating," he said with a grimace. "I might have known! Is this your usual bedtime fare, Green Eyes?"

"Not necessarily. Sometimes I read history. Or novels."

He put the book down on her bedside table. "That's a relief. What kind of novels?"

"Oh, all kinds," she said vaguely, trying not to notice that he was now sitting on the edge of her bed—and that, although he still had his jeans on, the top half of him was enticingly bare.

"Classics?" he suggested.

"Sometimes."

"What else?"

"Oh, mysteries, suspense, sagas..."

"No grope and grapple stuff?" He was grinning, and his eyes were teasing her, but somehow she didn't feel disturbed by his presence any more. It seemed quite normal that he should be here, laughing with her over her books.

"Sometimes that too," she admitted, grinning back. "What about you?"

"Me? Oh, my tastes are very sober. Strictly travel and business."

"You should try something different, then," she suggested, indicating the *Healthy* tome.

Aaron picked it up again, looking dubious. "Should I?" He swung one leg up on to the bed and settled himself beside her on the pillows. "Then why don't we read it together?"

She stole a quick glance at his face, but there was nothing in it to show that his suggestion was anything but innocent. All the same, she hadn't been born yesterday, and she had been married quite long enough to know that when a young and lusty man sat on your bed—and put his arm carelessly around your shoulders—he was likely to have a lot more on his mind than literature, however healthy.

But somehow it didn't seem to matter. She liked the feel of his arm around her, she liked his breath brushing her ear and, a short time later, she liked the touch of his lips against her forehead.

"It says here that sugar uses up nutrients already being digested in our bodies," said Emily, her eyes firmly on the open page on her lap.

"Does it? I'm not thinking of my digestion just at the moment."

"And it says excessive sugar consumption is associated with obesity, heart attacks, arthritis, ulcers and gout."

"Really?" said Aaron, putting his hand beneath the sheet and laying it lightly on her stomach.

"Really." She turned her cheek and rested it against his shoulder. "Aaron, what are you doing?"

"Exploring," he replied, moving his hand lower.

"Oh. I thought we were reading this book."

"Were we? I can think of better things to do." He bent his head and kissed the top of one of Mickey Mouse's ears. Outside in the hallway Biscuit grunted comfortably in his sleep.

"Aaron," murmured Emily, feeling light-headed and dizzy just as the book had said, "Aaron, we mustn't..."

"Of course not," he agreed, tugging gently at the hem of her nightshirt.

She moaned and buried her face in the tough, tanned skin of his chest. Gradually she felt the nightshirt slide up over her hips, and his hand curve gently around her bottom. He smelled musky and male and—oh, so achingly desirable...

At the back of her mind she was sure this was wrong, that it wasn't what she'd meant to happen at all. And yet it felt so right. She was drugged, intoxicated by the warmth of his body, by the purposeful movement of his hands and, as the nightshirt finally slipped over her head and disappeared on to the floor, by the feel of his lips on her breasts, her ears, her neck... His kisses trailed lightly around her chin until, at last, his mouth moved over hers. And she responded to it as perhaps she had wanted to from the moment she had first seen him standing on the dock at Gold River. They had kissed before, but never like this, with a slow, unhurried passion that she knew would move irresistibly on its course until it reached the point of no return.

Unless she stopped him.

Her hand reached down, touched the compact muscles of his thigh and returned with renewed purpose to his waist.

In a moment his jeans joined the nightshirt. So did most of the covers.

"Are you sure you wouldn't prefer to finish that book?" asked Aaron, his voice husky with laughing passion as he pushed her back on the pillows and rolled on top of her.

She stared into his eyes, felt the pressure of his strong thigh between her legs, and a flare of undeniable heat twisted inside her and made her gasp. "Book...?" she whispered. "I..." Her whispers faded into silence, and she shook her head.

"Thank heaven," he muttered. He smoothed her long hair on the pillow. "No, that's not right. Thank *you*, Emily my love. For being you."

His eyes were bright, smoldering with desire, and she knew that if she didn't stop him now, at once, this scene would be played out to its inescapable conclusion. The glorious, passionate conclusion that at this moment she longed for more than anything else in the world. She wanted to make love to Aaron. Now, with no further prevarication.

Healthy Eating clattered to the floor.

She didn't stop him.

And it was even more glorious than she'd imagined.

"Did you know that the best time to take amino-acid supplements is an hour or two after a workout?" asked Aaron.

His voice came to her out of a fog. She was lying in her own bed, of that she was sure, but something was different. And she felt drowsy, at peace, contented in a way she couldn't remember being for years. Something must have happened...

Aaron! She opened her eyes with a small gasp. He was sitting up in bed beside her, reading her book on health. At least he seemed to be reading it, because it was open on the covers in front of him and looking a bit the worse for wear. But his eyes weren't on the printed page. Instead they were smiling down into hers. "What?" she murmured dazedly. "Amino acids?"

He laughed softly and closed the book with a snap. "We're too late for them anyway," he assured her. "Do you realize it's nearly noon?"

"Oh!" cried Emily, struggling up on one elbow. "Oh, dear, the animals——"

"It's okay, sweetheart, I've looked after them. Why don't you lie down? I haven't made love to you for..." he looked at the gold and white clock "...five hours."

Emily collapsed weakly against the pillows as memories came crowding back. Maybe he hadn't made love to her for five hours, but she couldn't count the times he'd loved her last night. As she had loved him. Vaguely she recollected that she'd meant to say "no," *had* said "no," in fact, but that somewhere along the line she'd ended up saying "yes." More than once.

Did she regret it? Right now she didn't know. Lying here, smiling up at him, she felt wonderful. Alive, happy, ready to grasp life and make it hers. But she was afraid too. Because she could no longer conceal from herself that she loved Aaron.

She lifted her hand tenderly to his face. Last night—last night had been like no other night before. But then perhaps that wasn't altogether surprising. She and David had been so very young...

But if she loved Aaron—and she did—then that meant she was vulnerable again. It meant she would be hurt again. Not just if something happened, as it had with

David, but because at the end of the summer Aaron would leave. And she'd be alone, trying once more to build a life out of the ashes of love. She'd done that once already, and she didn't want to have to do it again.

A crow cawed raucously outside, and she closed her eyes. No, she might not want to do it again, but she had no choice, had she? The damage was done. Aaron was beside her grinning that impossible grin as he smoothed a finger softly down her side—and she loved him and must live for the moment.

Smiling, she held out her arms.

Two things stood out in the week that followed. The weather, which was unrelentingly wet, so that most of the time they stayed home to talk, argue over what to eat, and make love—and the final day when at last the sun came out.

Taking Biscuit, and Aaron's car, they headed optimistically for Little Qualicum Falls. There were only a few people walking along the woodland trails beside the river, and when they reached the spot where the water formed a swimming pool between the rocks it was deserted. In the distance they could hear the sound of the falls.

"Last one in gets to eat my carrot cake with carob icing!" shouted Emily, plunging into the crystal-clear water.

"Like hell," said Aaron from behind her, as he too leaped into the pool. "I've heard of sure winners, but I'm damned if I'm going to be a sure loser."

The icy cold of the snow-fed water closed around them, and after that Emily was too busy fighting to get back what was left of her breath to respond to his insults about her food.

She gasped as Aaron swept his arm around her and dragged her quickly back to the rocky shore.

"Brr!" she shuddered, snuggling against his cold, wet body. "Talk about taking one's breath away..."

Aaron ran his finger down her back. "I thought that was my province," he growled, pulling her to him and covering her mouth with his lips.

"Mmm," she murmured some time later, "I'll take you over the water any day. You're *much* warmer."

"You'd better believe I am." He pulled her on to a convenient rock and began to rub a towel over her shivering figure with a slow, deliberate sensuality.

"Oh!" gasped Emily, as Biscuit chose that moment to finish his swim, shake himself, and drench them in a shower of icy droplets.

"Bloody dog," muttered Aaron. "I told you to leave him at home."

"That's why I brought him," said Emily.

"You little..." He let the towel drop, and put his hands on her shoulders. "If I'd known that when I found your miserable mutt hitchhiking in the back of my car, I'd have thrown him out."

"You wouldn't. And he wasn't hitchhiking. I put him there."

"I see. You mean if I hadn't told you to you *would* have left him at home?" His eyes weren't quite so warm now, and his grip on her shoulders tightened.

"I might have. I'm not your daughter, Aaron. I don't have to do what you say."

"Oh, don't you? We'll see about that!"

Emily began to inch her way along the rock, because she read the promise of retaliation, as well as amusement, in his eyes. Then she gasped as she felt her upper body being bent relentlessly downward.

She never knew what would have happened next, because just before she lost her balance completely, she managed to choke out, "I suppose your wife was some little mouse who always obeyed her lord and master's orders."

At once he stopped pulling her over and pushed her upright. "My wife?" he said harshly. "My——Emily, I believe I've told you before, Tommy's mother is a subject we don't discuss."

"*You* don't discuss, you mean," she said, frowning. "Aaron, why——?"

"In the words of Mrs. Krowiak when Tommy gets on her nerves, 'Because I said so.' Is that clear enough for you?"

Oh, it was clear enough all right, and the sun was disappearing behind a big navy blue cloud. The wind shivered suddenly through the trees, and Emily jumped to her feet.

"It's going to rain," she said abruptly. "We'd better go home."

They didn't talk much after that, and by the time they got back to the cottage the rain was pelting down, so that in the dash between the car and the front door the two of them got thoroughly soaked. The third member of the party smelled like raw wet wool.

They headed straight into the bedroom and began to peel off their dripping clothes, not saying anything because the specter of Aaron's wife, and his strange reluctance to talk about her, hung between them.

Then their eyes met, held for a long moment, and suddenly they were in each other's arms.

The rest of their clothes dropped to the bedroom floor as they tumbled in a tangle of damp limbs onto the bed.

But when Emily lifted her head to nestle it snugly against Aaron's chest, her eye chanced to fall on the clock.

Time, she thought, with a shock of consternation. It was passing. And they couldn't ignore it much longer.

"Aaron," she murmured, her fingers lacing in his strong black hair. "Aaron, tomorrow——"

"There is no tomorrow," he said huskily. "Only now."

His hand was running deliciously up the inside of her thigh, he had lifted her half on top of him so that she could feel the hard angle of his hip, and with gentle pressure on the back of her head he was forcing her mouth down to his.

So for a while, as he had said, there was only now.

Some time later, though, as they lay damply entwined on the rumpled sheets, Emily's mind returned to the clock.

"Tommy," she said. "Aaron, Tommy's coming back tomorrow."

"So she is," he agreed laconically, lifting his head and kissing her nose.

"Yes, but that means—that means you can't stay here tonight."

"I don't see why not."

"Because we don't know what *time* she's coming back, and I'd hate her to find us—find us—well, like this."

"We'll set the alarm."

"Aaron, we've been setting the alarm every night since she left, and you always swear at it and shut it off." She smiled, a small, teasing smile. "And then after a while you stop swearing and——"

"Tomorrow I won't," he promised, grinning. "But tonight..." His hand moved up to cup her breast.

"You know you will. I'm serious, Aaron. I won't be able to sleep at all if I think Tommy may arrive home to find us—you know..."

"Mmm," he agreed with a reminiscent leer, "indeed I do know. That's why I have no intention of abandoning this bed before midnight. But, if you insist, I suppose I could sleep on the sofa."

"I think the Inn would be safer."

"The Inn be damned!" His voice wasn't lazy now, and he propped himself up on one elbow to fix her with a stern glare. "Emily, this nonsense has gone far enough. I've been holding back, not saying anything because I didn't want to scare you away..." The muscles in his throat moved convulsively. "And because the last time I asked a woman——"

"What do you mean?" she interrupted, gazing at him with puzzlement and a little fear. "What haven't you said?"

"Dammit, that I love you and I want to marry you!" His voice came out in a roar, his breath blasting over her face. "And if you think I'm spending the night at any inn, you can bloody well think again!" He emphasized the point with a ferocious scowl.

"Oh," said Emily, moistening her lips and wondering why her brain had gone numb.

David had proposed to her too, long ago, she thought vaguely. But not like this. Not leaning over her, all naked and sexy and shouting, and with a look on his face that was more suited to murder than marriage.

But this man wasn't David. And she couldn't think. Not with him looking like that... Had he really said he loved her?

"But you can't," she whispered. "You don't mean it, surely? It's just that Tommy——"

"Tommy has nothing to do with it," he said roughly. "And I do mean it. I meant it the first day I met you on the *Uchuck*. But you didn't believe me."

"What?" said Emily blankly. "You couldn't have. You were joking."

"I wasn't joking. I didn't expect you to accept, but if you had I'd have married you. I could see that you were right for Tommy, who needs a mother. I had a feeling you'd suit me very nicely in bed..." he stopped scowling and patted her bottom absently "...which you do, and, although I thought your personality left some room for improvement—a bit of whipping into shape, so to speak—I figured I could handle it. So I certainly wasn't joking."

"Oh!" Emily wriggled away from him, swung her legs out of bed, and stormed across to the wardrobe. Grabbing at the first thing she could lay her hands on, she pulled on a long white T-shirt that just about covered her thighs. When she swung around, Aaron was lying back on the bed with his hands behind his head, and the sheet lurking distractingly around his hipbones. His eyes were moving over her with warm approval. And he was grinning.

"Well?" he asked, quirking an eyebrow.

"Well, *what*?" she demanded.

"Will you marry me?"

She stared at him, and came to the stunned conclusion that he was serious. Somewhere along the line there, she seemed to remember he had actually said he loved her. But apart from that, his proposal had been on a par—no, considerably more offensive—than Mr. Darcy's first proposal to Elizabeth Bennet. And that was after assuring her that he didn't want to scare her away.

"No," she said, not allowing herself time to think.

Aaron stopped grinning and sat up. "Emily, I was trying to tell you the truth. I can't tell you it was love at first sight. But it was *like* enough at first sight to make me follow you to Cinnamon Bay. If I hadn't had the good fortune to come upon you wrestling with your thug, I'd planned to find a room here and track you down. I knew you thought I was an arrogant bastard, but I hoped——"

"You hoped you'd get me into bed."

"Of course. But I hoped for a lot more than that. For instance, that when we got to know each other..." He shrugged, and when he spoke again his voice was surprisingly bitter. "I guess I hoped I'd finally found a woman I could love. Who might love me. I haven't had much luck in that line up to now. I suppose that could be because I haven't tried recently." He shrugged again. "Besides, not many women are willing to put up with Tommy. Then I met you, and I had this foolish fancy." He stopped abruptly, his features hardening. "Stupid of me. When Hatton showed up, I figured I'd made a mistake."

"So you left to have breakfast," said Emily, keeping her eyes resolutely on his face because this wasn't the time to let her gaze stray lower.

"A man must eat, a fact of life which you seem to have difficulty accepting," he said dryly. "Besides, I came back, didn't I?"

"Only because you couldn't stand the thought of someone else getting something you wanted."

"No, that was only one reason." He turned his head to stare grimly out at the rain, and she knew he was light years away from her now, somewhere in the past where she couldn't follow. But when he turned back to her he held out his hand.

"Come here, Emily," he ordered quietly. "Don't sulk. I know that wasn't the world's most romantic proposal. But I do love you, and, unless I'm very much mistaken, you love me. So..." he took a deep breath, and smiled crookedly "...so let's get married. Because I don't want to listen to any more nonsense about inns."

Emily shook her head, not sure her ears were doing their job. But her head seemed clear now, and Aaron was sitting up in the bed looking as impossibly desirable as ever. And he obviously expected an answer.

"That," she said, enunciating each word carefully, "is the worst apology for a proposal I've ever heard."

Aaron stopped smiling. "I haven't had much practice," he answered shortly.

"I can tell."

He frowned. "Emily, are you going to marry me or not?"

She pursed her lips, and two small lines appeared between her eyebrows. This didn't add up. Aaron was nobody's fool, he had a way with words when it suited him—and it certainly ought to suit him now—but he was acting like a man with no sensitivity to anyone's needs but his own. A man who, apparently, believed that all he had to do was inform her he wanted to marry her, and that would be an end to the matter. It was odd, really, not in character with the Aaron she had loved and laughed with all this week. It was almost as if his sudden gruffness was a facade he'd assumed to mask what he really felt.

But watching him now, Emily knew what *she* felt. She loved him. And he had asked her to marry him. The question was, was she ready to take the risk? In a way she wanted to, because now she couldn't imagine a life without him. But in another way she was afraid, haunted by the memory of David, and confused and disturbed by Aaron's bluntness.

"Come here," he said again, when she didn't move.

Slowly, almost as if she were walking to her doom instead of to the man who loved her, she moved toward him. When she was close enough, he leaned forward to catch her hands, drawing her down to him till she was perched on the edge of the bed.

"Well?" His eyes on her face were very still.

"I—I don't know." She lowered her head, unable to bear that dark, shadowed gaze on her face. "I don't know, Aaron."

He put his hand under her chin and made her look at him. "Don't you love me?"

"I——Yes. Yes, I love you." She felt a ridiculous lump in her throat, and when he removed his hand she let her forehead drop on to his shoulder.

He moved his fingers to the back of her head, ruffling her hair. "Then what's the problem, Green Eyes?" he demanded. His voice was rough, not letting her off the hook. "Are you still running away?"

"Maybe," she admitted in a muffled voice. "But it's not just that, it's..." She stopped, not knowing how to tell him that she suspected there were things he wasn't telling her, things that could hurt her in a way she never wanted to be hurt again. With David it had been different. She'd known him for years, and there had been no danger of unpleasant surprises.

"I don't know," she repeated. "Give me time, Aaron."

"All right," he said, brusque now to the point of indifference, "I'll give you time. I don't have much choice, do I? Short of slinging you over my shoulder, locking you up, and keeping you on bread and water till you say 'yes.'"

Emily giggled, as a wave of relief washed over her. She could put off the moment of decision a while longer. "Would you do that?" she asked shakily.

"I might," he replied, his tone so grim that she felt uncomfortable again.

But after that it was time to think about supper, and they fell into their usual pattern of sparring over the contents of Emily's cupboards and Aaron's carnivorous taste in food. Fleetingly, it occurred to her that if she ever seriously considered marrying him this source of permanent friction would have to be dealt with. Then she stopped worrying about it, because he was kissing the back of her neck as she wrestled to open a package of whole-wheat pasta.

That night, as the last shivers of bliss faded into warm contentment, Aaron put his arms around Emily, closed his eyes, and prepared to go to sleep.

Emily dug him sharply in the ribs. "Out," she said. "You promised you'd sleep on the sofa."

"I was drunk at the time, so it doesn't count," he murmured drowsily.

"No, you weren't. We came straight in from the rain and went to bed."

"Sensible of us."

"Aaron! You have to go."

He wrapped his arm more securely around her waist and told her not to be tiresome.

"But, Aaron—Tommy..."

He lifted himself up on his elbow and gazed down at her face in the moonlight. "Emily, my love," he said bluntly, "you're a very troublesome woman, who worries too much about other people's daughters."

"Please," she said, trying not to sound like a child begging for a treat. "I won't be able to sleep if you stay."

"I'm not sure I want you to sleep," he said, laying a possessive hand over her breast.

"Aaron..."

Aaron, catching the note of desperation in her voice, gave an exasperated laugh and said disgustedly, "Oh, for heaven's sake, Green Eyes! You worry too much. All right, if it will make you happy, I'll go. This time."

"It will make me happy," said Emily. "Thank you."

"It is *not* my pleasure," Aaron assured her, slouching out of the room to spend the next fifteen minutes crashing around setting up his bed. Emily knew quite well he was doing it on purpose to annoy her, but in fact it only made her smile.

But after the noise had died down, and she found herself on her own for the first time in a week, she didn't feel happy, as she had told him she would. She felt unexpectedly forlorn and bereft.

It took her a long time to get to sleep, but she still woke early. At first she wasn't sure what had woken her, so she rolled over, her hand reaching automatically for Aaron.

He wasn't there, but when she opened sleep-drugged eyes to look around the room, she saw that somebody else was.

Andrew Hatton, his big face only inches from her own, was leaning over the bed. His hand was on her shoulder, beginning to shake it, and when she drew in her breath in a horrified gulp she practically passed out from the overpowering smell of stale whisky.

CHAPTER EIGHT

"ANDREW!" gasped Emily. "What are you doing? Where—how?"

"Wanna talk to you, love." His voice was slurred, thickened to an alcoholic mumble.

"Where's Yvonne?" she asked, pulling the sheet up around her neck. "I thought you two were in Yellowknife."

"Was. Came home. She's not spe—speaking to me. Wanna talk about it."

"Oh," said Emily. "I see." She thought for a moment, wondering how best to handle this situation. "Listen, Andrew, I'll be glad to talk to you, but not now. First you go home and get some sleep——"

"Sleep?" interrupted a coldly furious voice from the doorway. "He'll be sleeping all right if he's not out of here in ten seconds!"

Andrew blinked owlishly, stood up and pivoted around to face the source of this threat.

"Huh," he grunted. "Silverstone. Thought you'd gone. Now listen, fella——" He stabbed his finger at Aaron and swayed toward him.

"No," said Aaron, in a tone that might have raised the hair on Andrew's scalp if he'd been sober. "*You* listen. I want you out of here—now. You've got exactly eight seconds left."

"You th-threatening me?" Andrew took a drunken step forward, not recognizing the precariousness of his position.

"No," replied Aaron, still in that terrifyingly cold voice, "I don't threaten."

"Andrew!" cried Emily, sitting up and forgetting that she was wearing a transparent white nightgown that left nothing to the imagination. "Andrew, please go. We'll have a long talk later on, when you're feeling better. And, Aaron, please stop looking like Mephistopheles, and let him pass."

Andrew lumbered around to face her, shook his head, and said foggily. "You wan me to go?"

"Yes, please."

"Huh." He stared, seeming to take in her attire—or lack of it—for the first time. "Oh, got it. Bad timing." He gave her a lopsided leer, and veered back toward the door. "Okay, love—going."

"Aaron," said Emily warningly, as Aaron's fists started to bunch up, "let him go."

She saw his eyes narrow and his nostrils flare, and for a moment she thought her plea would be ignored. But after a second's hesitation, and with what appeared to be a superhuman exercise in control, he stood aside and allowed Andrew to stumble out into the hall.

The front door slammed, and the two of them were alone except for Buster, who was sitting on Emily's dressing table looking sphinx-like.

Emily had been following Andrew's erratic progress across the floor, but now she turned cautiously to Aaron.

His face was much paler than usual, and the line of his mouth quite brutal.

"Aaron," she said quietly, "there's no reason to look like that. No harm's been done. Andrew's had a fight with Yvonne, that's all, and he's obviously been drowning his troubles. He just wanted someone to unload on."

"No doubt," replied Aaron through his teeth. "But why you? And why the *hell* has he still got your key?"

Emily sighed. This wasn't going to be one of the greatest mornings she'd ever had. "I expect he wanted to talk to me because I'm a friend of Yvonne's. And he has my key because he's very good about looking after the animals while I'm out. I told you that."

"So you did. But you're not out. You're here, with me."

"Yes, but you won't always be here."

The look that passed over his face then frightened Emily. His jaw clenched and his eyes blazed as if she'd struck him. And he was more than just angry. For a moment she thought he meant to hit back. Then all she could see on his set features was a bitterness so deep that it made her blanch. When he strode across the room to bend over her with his fists punched into the mattress on either side of her hips, she shrank back against the pillows.

He gave a snort of contempt. "For heaven's sake, do you honestly think I'm going to hurt you?" he demanded.

She thought it entirely possible, judging from the grating savagery with which he spoke. But she decided it wouldn't be politic to say so. She had known right from the beginning that Aaron could be dangerous company, and just now the danger quivered in the air with an almost tangible tension.

"No, of course not," she replied, clutching the sheet with both hands because she needed something to hold on to.

"Well, that's a start." He moved his face closer. "Now tell me what you meant by that remark."

"What remark?" Emily swallowed, her eyes riveted on the cleft in his chin.

"You said I wouldn't always be here." His voice was controlled now, but only barely. "Or had you forgotten?"

"No. No, I—it's just that you'll be going back to Boston."

"If I do, you'll be coming with me. Won't you?" It was more of a warning than a question.

"But this is my home. I have a job here."

"There are jobs in Boston. But I'm not all that wedded to the idea of spending my life there. We can work something out." Aaron spoke tightly, with an obvious effort to keep his temper.

She could feel his breath steaming on her cheek, and his bare chest was almost touching hers. The only small mercy was that he had stopped to pull on jeans before bursting in to slay his dragon in the person of Andrew Hatton.

"Aaron, you said you'd give me time," she protested.

"I've given you time. As of this morning, it's run out."

"Because of Andrew? But Andrew means nothing to me. He never did."

"I know that. But I *don't* know what you mean to him, and I'm not going back to Boston leaving that drunken lout to wander into your house whenever he feels like it. Especially not when he's likely to find you looking like this." He hooked his fingers possessively into the front of her filmy nightgown and sat down abruptly on the bed. "If I do go back alone, Emily, believe me, it will be because I'm not coming back."

"But——"

"No, not but. I mean it. Do you understand?"

"Yes," whispered Emily, "I understand. Only—Andrew doesn't have to keep the key, you know. If that would set your mind at rest——"

"What would set my mind at rest would be knowing you're my wife. For the last time, Emily, will you marry me?" She saw signs of an inner struggle, before he added curtly, "Please."

"I—I don't know." She stared up into the face of the man she loved, so hard now, so implacable. Could she marry him? It was no longer just a matter of overcoming her fear of being hurt. It was Aaron himself. Suddenly he was impossibly domineering, as well as autocratic and harsh. He had always had an arrogant streak, but beneath the arrogance had been a gentleness which she had come to expect. And now he was demanding an answer from her. At once. But she was used to taking her time, to making her own independent decisions . . .

Sighing, she stared out of the window, not wanting to see that demanding glitter in his eyes. It disturbed her, because at this moment he was showing classic signs of being the sort of tyrannical male who would expect to make all her decisions for her.

She could never let him do that.

He put his hand on her cheek, making her face tingle, and for one fleeting instant she wanted desperately to reach out, to push her fingers into his hair and pull his mouth down to hers. But she couldn't do it. Her arms wouldn't make the move.

"I don't think I can marry you, Aaron," she said at last, the words dragging out of her in a thin whisper. "I love you. But I'm used to my independence now, to being my own boss, doing things my way. So are you, and I don't think—well, I don't think it would work."

Aaron straightened very slowly, and when she saw the expression in his eyes she wanted to cry out that she hadn't meant it, that of course she would marry him. But she couldn't cry out, because her throat had closed up, and no words came—and because as well as pain, and a kind of haunted anguish, there was a fierce rigidity about the way he was looking at her now, an inflexibility that seemed to come not from a desire to mask his feelings, but from something cold and uncompromising deep inside. It was anger too, she thought, watching the way his lip curled. But not any ordinary anger caused by hurt. She remembered his hard reticence about his marriage, about that other woman he must once have loved. And she was certain that this anger came from something he had lived with for a long time.

He stood up, moving to the foot of the bed and grasping the brass rail as if he wanted to break it.

"Is that your answer?" he asked with such devastating detachment that she cringed. "I won't ask you again."

"I..." She stared at him, feeling as if her heart were being crushed in a vice, and then broken into a thousand minute fragments. "I..."

She couldn't say it. She couldn't say that no, it wasn't her answer, that she only wanted more time. Because he wouldn't give her time. And even if he did, she was sure that in the end her answer would be the same. Aaron was too dangerous a man to marry. The way he was acting now only emphasized the rightness of her decision.

"I'm sorry," she whispered, through lips that seemed suddenly cracked. "I can't, Aaron—I can't!"

She turned her face into the pillow, so she wouldn't have to watch him leave.

But when she felt his hand close over her shoulder she remembered that he couldn't just walk out on her. Her closet was full of his clothes. And Tommy would be back some time today.

"Emily? I'm afraid you'll have to get up. The Oliphants mentioned catching an early ferry, and we've wasted more time than we should have." Still that heart-breaking detachment, almost as if he didn't care that the time they had "wasted" involved the shattering of dreams she hadn't even realized she had.

"Right," she said, her voice muffled by the pillow, "I'll get dressed."

She did, but in a tear-misted fog that prevented her from seeing or caring that she was putting on her black shirt with the pocket half ripped off, the khaki shorts that she normally kept for painting walls or bathing Biscuit, and one blue and one white sock.

When she went out into the kitchen, she found Aaron there scraping charcoal off four slices of burnt toast.

"I made breakfast," he said, throwing them on to a plate, and apparently not appreciating the irony.

Emily remembered how she would have teased him about it, even yesterday, and she didn't appreciate the joke either.

They munched the charred remains in grim silence, watched by an ever-hopeful Biscuit. When Emily could stand it no longer, she asked hesitantly, "Are you leaving, Aaron? When Tommy gets back?"

He made a sound that wasn't quite a laugh. "What do you expect me to do?"

"You could stay. We're still friends, aren't we?"

"No," said Aaron, so harshly that Emily jumped. "I am not your friend, Emily. I'm your lover. And I can't stay here watching you, wanting you, and knowing I can never have you except for a few snatched, sleazy little moments when we've managed to get rid of Tommy. Apart from which, my daughter is much too bright not to catch on to what's happening. Assuming that's what you're suggesting."

Emily didn't know what she was suggesting. She only knew she couldn't bear to lose him. But he was right. It would be impossible for both of them if he stayed.

"No," she said, staring at the burnt crumbs on her plate. "No, I guess I'm not suggesting that."

"Which is why I'm leaving," he said shortly. "And now, if you don't mind, I'd better pack."

She minded desperately. But she couldn't say so. She could only watch in silent anguish as he threw his belongings together along with some of Tommy's paraphernalia, and then loaded the lot into his car. Not once while he was doing it did he look at her, and by the time he had finished she was almost ready to scream. She wanted to run across the gravel, pound him on the chest and shout at him that it was all his fault.

But she knew it wasn't, and she almost wished he would turn on her, threaten her or do something physical, just so that she would have a reason to hate him.

When the last bag had been stuffed into the trunk, he finally turned to face her.

She was leaning against the doorframe, watching him, her long hair blowing in the breeze. Aaron's eyes stayed on her, steady and watchful, taking in the torn shirt and mismatched socks. "I'll miss you, Emily," he said, with a lack of emphasis that made it sound as if he were saying he'd miss a discontinued brand of shampoo. "Thank you for..." He gestured helplessly at the cottage.

"For having you?" she suggested bitterly. "It's been a—a..." She was trying to say "pleasure," but her tongue wouldn't get around the word. Abruptly she spun on her heel and ran back into the house.

She half expected he would follow, but he didn't, and about ten minutes later, with a lot of door slamming and laughter, she heard the Oliphants deliver Tommy.

Then she heard their car pull away. After that there was a long silence, and she was just beginning to wonder if both Aaron and Tommy could possibly have left without her hearing the car start, when Tommy came quietly into the bedroom, to find her hostess gazing blankly at the big, unruffled bed.

"Dad says we have to go," she said, not sulkily, but as if she was trying to hold back tears. "He says you've got visitors coming. But it's not true, is it? I can tell from that funny look in his eyes." She sighed. "I bet we don't get to spend more than one night any place on the way home. We never do when he's in a bad mood. He has to keep moving on."

Emily tried to smile. "I hope he won't be in a bad mood, Tommy, and I'm sorry you have to go." She kept her voice level with a great effort.

"It's all right," replied Tommy. "We can write, to each other, can't we? I like writing letters. My friend Margaret says I'm crazy."

"Of course we can." Emily didn't hesitate, even though she knew it would be torture to write to Aaron's child, knowing she would never see either of them again.

"And maybe we can come back next summer?" suggested Tommy.

"Um—yes. Yes, I hope so."

"Mmm." Tommy studied her with big, perceptive eyes. "I hoped you and Dad would get married," she announced candidly. "But you're not going to, are you? And *that's* why we're going home."

Tommy hadn't been getting straight As for nothing.

"Something like that," admitted Emily, smiling wanly. "But you and I can still be friends."

"But not you and Dad?"

"Oh, we're still friends too."

They weren't, though. Aaron had refused to be her friend.

Five minutes later, after Aaron had brushed off Emily's offer of lunch, the three of them stood in the clearing in front of the cottage going through the motions of polite leave-taking.

Aaron's face was shadowed by the trees as he took her hand, held it for a moment, and then bent forward to kiss her on the cheek. When she felt his lips touch her skin, Emily drew in her breath, and at once he dropped her fingers as if he had mistakenly picked up a particularly repellent reptile.

"Goodbye, and thank you," he said formally, inclining his head.

"Yes, *thank* you," echoed Tommy, with far more enthusiasm. "I'll write to you soon. At the same time as I write to Caroline Oliphant."

When Emily smiled, Tommy ran over to give her an impulsive hug. Emily hugged her back, biting her lip, and blinking to keep the tears from spilling over.

"Come on, Tommy!" called Aaron impatiently. He was already swinging his long legs into the station wagon.

Tommy gave her a last quick hug and jumped in too.

Emily raised her hand in automatic farewell as Aaron started the engine and turned to roll down the window. Their eyes met, and in that brief exchange it seemed that everything they had ever been to each other was expressed, wordlessly and without any need for speech. All the same, she opened her mouth. But whatever she might have said was drowned out by the roar of the engine. Then the station wagon was bumping down the lane, and as it vanished around a bend Emily realized she was still holding her arm in the air. She frowned at it, then lowered it quickly as a drop of rain fell on her upturned face.

Slowly, walking like an old woman, she dragged herself back to the cottage, past a faintly puzzled Buster and Biscuit, and into the bedroom she had shared with Aaron. The bedroom she would never share with any man again.

When she flung herself down on the covers, she didn't even notice that the rain had soaked her through to the skin.

A long time later Buster padded over to the bed, flicked his tail, and jumped up to curl himself against her chest. When he didn't move in spite of her dampness, she put her arm around him, grateful for this small soft crumb of comfort.

"Emily, for the sake of *my* sanity, if not for your own, will you please get in touch with that bloody man and put things right?"

Yvonne sat with her feet up on Emily's coffee table, glaring at her friend over the top of a large glass of lemonade, and waving a newspaper vaguely in the direction of a buzzing fly.

"He's not a bloody man, and I can't put things right," replied Emily, closing her eyes and wishing the rain would return in all its dreariness. It would be easier to take than this heat, and much better suited to her mood.

"Why not?" demanded Yvonne, sounding belligerent.

"Because even if I wanted to get in touch with Aaron, which I don't, I wouldn't have the slightest idea where to find him. He doesn't have to be home until school starts. It's his company, so he can take whatever time off he wants."

"Oh." Yvonne pursed her lips. "I suppose that's a bit of a problem."

"Yes," sighed Emily, "I'm afraid it is."

Not that she wanted to get in touch with Aaron, she thought wearily. At least she did, but she wasn't going to. Nothing had changed because he'd left. He was still the same dangerous man she'd tried to run away from on the very first day they had met. A man who demanded what he wanted and expected to get it. A man who had shattered her hard-won tranquillity when he moved in to take over her life. And now she must fight to win back that peace and tranquillity. *Had* been fighting for the past three weeks. But it was a battle she didn't really expect to win. After a long time, she had recovered from the burden of David's death. But Aaron wasn't David. He wasn't dead either, she acknowledged grimly. And she longed for him, hungered for him and needed him, as she had never needed anyone in her life.

"Stop dreaming and do something about it," advised Yvonne. "You're losing weight, you know, and you're one of those lucky beasts who can't afford to."

Emily started. She had been so far away she had forgotten her friend was in the room. It had been three weeks to the day since Aaron and Tommy had left. In that time Yvonne and Andrew had made up their quarrel—which inevitably had involved Andrew's attentions to an exceptionally pretty redhead from Yellowknife—and announced that they planned to get married. Privately, Emily thought her friend would have her hands full, but she didn't say so, because if anyone could cope with Andrew it would be Yvonne. In truth, Emily was so mired in her own unhappiness, in the feeling that from now on her life would be stagnant and dead, that she didn't feel up to wrestling with anyone's problems but her own.

She wasn't doing such a hot job with those either, as Yvonne had had no hesitation in pointing out.

"There isn't much I *can* do about it," Emily explained listlessly. "Aaron's gone, I don't know where he is, and, even if I did, there are things I don't understand about him, don't really trust. I still think we're wrong for each other."

"Perhaps," agreed Yvonne, swirling the lemonade in her glass. "But there's no such thing as perfection." She made a face. "I should know. Thing is, if you love each other—which, judging from that dismal face of yours, you do—I don't see why you can't make a go of it." She swung her legs to the floor and jumped up. "Anyway, everything's a risk. No point in hiding back here in the woods because of that—much too dull. You think about it." She bounced over to the door, announcing that Andrew was waiting for her to cook dinner because he was too lazy to do it for himself.

"And you let him get away with that?" asked Emily, surprised.

"Only sometimes." Yvonne grinned, and bustled off down the lane.

After she had gone, Emily did think about it. Not because Yvonne had told her to, but because she had been thinking about very little else since Aaron had left.

She was still thinking about it on a bright and breezy day in September, four weeks later, as she sat on a log scuffing her toes in the sand, and watching the white-caps flake foam over the stained green glass of the ocean. Three days ago she had returned from a brief visit to her mother which she had hoped would take her mind off her heartache.

It hadn't.

In the seven agonizing weeks since she had bid that strained goodbye to Aaron, Emily had come to know exactly what she had lost. She had lost the love of a strong, vital man whose humor and laughter and caring had brought joy and a different meaning to her quiet, uneventful existence. Aaron had taught her to feel again, to care for another person more than she cared for herself. If she had only known it. He had given her his body, shown her the miracle that physical love could be when two people wanted only to make each other happy. But, more than that, he had taught her that these same two very different people could learn to accept and take pleasure in their differences. Because they loved each other.

But she had lost all that. No, she corrected herself, picking up a handful of sand and watching it scatter in the breeze. No, she hadn't lost it. She had thrown it away. And up until a few days ago there had been nothing she could have done about it. But now Aaron would be back in Boston. She could, if she had the courage, pick up the phone and call him...

"Biscuit!" she shouted abruptly. "Come on, boy! We're going home." Relinquishing her perch on the log, Emily took a last look at the turbulent sea sparkling in the autumn sun, and made her way steadily back up the hill.

Half an hour later she stood in the hallway of the cottage staring down at her plain black phone. It had mysteriously assumed the shape of a monster. A monster whose name, she knew, was Risk.

It was a full four minutes before she closed her eyes, seized the phone, and began to dial Information. In the end, she got the wrong number, and another two minutes had passed before the phone at last began to ring in Boston. It rang thirteen times.

No one was home.

Emily put the receiver back on its stand with a feeling that, she was ashamed to admit, was partly relief. Aaron and Tommy were out. Maybe the smartest thing to do would be to send a letter.

"Easiest thing to do too," she muttered, out loud, causing Biscuit to prick up his ears.

As it turned out, she wasn't altogether right about that. The letter was anything but easy to write. She started it half a dozen times, not knowing how to tell him that she wasn't sure, but she thought she'd made a terrible mistake. Aaron hadn't taken it at all kindly the last time she'd said she wasn't sure.

In the end she just wrote, "I miss you and I love you. If you still love me, please write." Then she licked the envelope, which tasted curiously sweet, and hurried to the Post Office before she could change her mind.

She knew she couldn't expect a reply before Tuesday, but on Monday she was at the Post Office again, hoping that just this once the mail service would take her by surprise.

It didn't.

She wasn't particularly concerned when there was no letter on Tuesday or Wednesday either, but, when nothing had come by Friday, she began to wonder.

The following Friday she opened her mailbox without much hope, to find only a collection of bills, a letter from her mother, and three requests for donations. It was two weeks now since she'd written to Aaron, and she knew that the time had come to face the truth she had been so desperately trying to avoid.

"Yvonne," she said to the little blonde later that evening, "it's obvious what's happened. Aaron's had plenty of time to think in the weeks since we were together. He's probably come to the conclusion that he made a mistake when he asked me to marry him. Followed, from his point of view, by a lucky escape."

"Nonsense," retorted Yvonne. "He'll write—you'll see."

Emily shook her head. "No," she said. "No, he won't. Not now. There isn't going to be any letter for me from Boston."

Yvonne, seeing the aching emptiness in her friend's eyes, blinked hurriedly and didn't answer.

CHAPTER NINE

EMILY munched a sandwich and glanced indifferently out of the window. It was November now, but the day was unseasonably bright, and Biscuit was lying in a sunbeam on the grass. As she watched, Buster stalked up behind him, paused for a moment, and began to bat his paw at the flopped-over tip of a furry ear. When Biscuit opened an eye, he batted again. The dog, heaving a visible sigh, lumbered to his feet and padded resignedly to the back door of the cottage.

Emily let him in, and immediately wished she hadn't. Her nose told her that somewhere in between breakfast and lunch he had located his version of doggy heaven—a delectably malodorous patch of compost. And of course he had rolled in it.

She sighed. Bathtime again. This was all she needed!

But as she ran the water into the bath, she reflected wryly that it might just as well be all she needed. It was Saturday, there was nothing important that had to be done, and no particular reason to do it anyway. There had seemed no particular reason to do anything since early August—although she *had* made an effort to reduce her kitchen clutter. She wasn't sure what had made her do that. Eventually, she supposed, she would get over Aaron, and regain the measure of contentment she had known before he came. But it hadn't happened yet, and at the back of her mind was a desolate, hollow, rather horrifying feeling that it never would. There was a new little girl at school too, who reminded her achingly of Tommy...

Biscuit was barking to go out again, not trusting the sound of running water, and Emily told herself firmly to stop moping and get on with the job.

Some time later, with a damp and reproachful dog glaring up at her from the mat, Emily, still very damp herself, stood by the kitchen table staring at her half-eaten sandwich. The house was unusually quiet. There had been a wind earlier, but it had died down now, and in the distance she could hear the sound of traffic humming busily along the beach. Then she heard another engine, closer, at the end of the lane. It sounded familiar.

She didn't move, couldn't move, any more than she could take her eyes off the sandwich.

A car door slammed, and she put both hands flat on the table. If she hadn't, she knew she would have fallen. Footsteps pounded across the gravel and someone knocked perfunctorily on the door. Had she locked it? She couldn't remember, she'd been getting more and more forgetful of late.

Apparently she hadn't, because the knock was followed by the sound of the door opening. Emily tried to turn her head, but her neck had gone inexplicably rigid. The footsteps were in the kitchen now.

Then strong hands were on her shoulders and that voice she had never expected to hear again remarked with a slight quiver in it, "You're wet. Isn't this where I came in?"

Emily gave a choked little sob as Aaron turned her around and pulled her very gently into his arms.

"That sandwich," he went on, stroking her damp back and gazing over the top of her head. "I believe we've met before too, haven't we? But I think it's dead."

Emily choked again, on a gurgle of laughter this time instead of a sob. "You haven't changed," she murmured, lifting her head from his chest and staring dazedly into the well-remembered eyes. "You're as rude as ever."

"Am I?" His voice was soft, caressing. "You haven't changed either. You're still wet. Is it a permanent condition?"

"Oh, Aaron!" Emily put her arms round his neck, not knowing whether to laugh or cry, and doing both. "I've been bathing Biscuit again. He rolled in something unspeakable."

"Mmm-hmm. And what else is new since I left?" He raised a sardonic eyebrow.

"Oh, Aaron," she repeated, "you're—you're horrible!" He wasn't, though. In his dark blue shirt, and with his face covered in dark stubble, he was the most beautiful sight she had ever seen. And his mockery was music to her ears.

"No, I'm not," he contradicted her. "In fact, I've frequently been assured I'm quite attractive."

Doubt and uncertainty thumped inside her chest. "You have?" she asked, with an unworthy stab of jealousy.

"Mostly by you."

She stopped feeling jealous at once and opened her mouth.

"No, don't say '"Oh, Aaron"' again," he said quickly. "I've got a better idea."

His lips closed over hers.

And he was right. It was a very much better idea.

When he at last took his mouth from hers, Emily's gaze strayed instinctively to the bedroom, where the door stood open and inviting across the hall. But he caught the direction of her eyes and shook his head.

"No," he said. "That's what got us into trouble before. Too much loving and not enough talking." He twisted a lock of her hair and tugged it gently. "Which was mostly my fault, I admit. So now why don't you make yourself something respectable to eat—no, not that dried-out abomination!" he exclaimed, removing the nearly extinct sandwich from her hand. "And then we'll sit down and talk." He laid particular emphasis on the "sit."

Emily reached for the butter. "Have *you* had lunch?" she asked.

"Yes. Thank goodness."

She sighed, reflecting with reluctant amusement that she had spoken the truth when she'd told Aaron he hadn't changed. And he was still determined to boss her around. But just for today it didn't seem to matter, because she wasn't capable of thinking straight anyway. She was too dazed, ecstatic, scared and happy to think. Especially happy.

With a meekness which she suspected surprised him, she made herself a fresh sandwich. He waited impatiently while she ate it, then put his arm around her and led her purposefully out of the kitchen.

"You're still wet," he observed, hesitating beside the striped sofa. "Don't you want to change out of those shorts?"

She did, but she didn't want him telling her what to do, so she said, "No."

He grinned. "Good. Wet suits you."

Emily glared, and his features sobered quickly as he sat down, pulling her with him.

"I missed you too, Green Eyes," he said, picking up her hand, and getting down to brass tacks with unnerving abruptness. "And yes, of course I still love you. But I couldn't write."

"You got my letter," she whispered, edging away from him as his knees brushed against her thigh. "I knew you had. But I thought—I thought..."

"You thought I wouldn't answer." His tone was accusing, and his grip on her hand tightened. "Did you really believe my love was as shallow as that?"

"No," she replied in a low voice. "I believed you thought you'd made a mistake. That you despised me because I was afraid to make a permanent commitment. Only I wasn't really. Not by then." She swallowed and fixed her gaze on the carpet. "But I *was* afraid of what we'd do to each other. You were so demanding and dictatorial there at the end, and I didn't think I could be happy with someone I didn't understand, someone who wanted to make my decisions for me—and who—who would never talk about his marriage..."

She stopped, because Aaron's face had a closed look about it now, and his fingers were digging into her palm.

"Go on," he said grimly. "What made you write to me, then?"

She stared at him, her eyes swimming with unshed tears. "I missed you," she said simply. "I didn't want to go on without you."

At once his features softened. He took a deep breath, saw what his fingers were doing, and guiltily began to smooth the marks on her hand. "You mean there's a chance that you'll have me?" he said. "Dictatorial and demanding as I am?"

He was pinning her to the sofa with those eyes. But they weren't demanding. They were intense, agonized, and she knew it was all he could do to keep himself from reaching out to grab her, to shake from her the answer he needed to hear. The answer she still hesitated to give.

But if she didn't, what hope was there? For either of them?

"Yes," she said, on a fading sigh. "Yes, Aaron, there's a chance."

His taut body relaxed very slowly, as the intensity of his gaze melted into tender warmth. "Thank you," he said, and for the second time that day he took her into his arms and kissed her with such passion that she thought her heart would break from joy and hope.

When he finally let her go, Emily pushed herself determinedly away from him and leaned back gasping. He smiled, and she longed to reach for him again. But she mustn't. Needing something to do with her hands, she began to smooth them over her shorts, and discovered they were almost dry. No wonder, she thought, laughing inwardly. Aaron's passion had always had the power to heat up everything it touched.

He was standing up now, moving resolutely to the easy chair. "It won't work," he observed, his mouth twisting crookedly.

"What won't?" She supposed the fear showed in her eyes, but she couldn't help it.

"Any attempt to talk while you're sitting there all wet and alluring beside me."

"Actually I'm more or less dry," she said, her heart thudding with relief. "So you shouldn't have any problem at all."

"Don't count on it."

"I won't," said Emily, with equanimity. "What is it you want to tell me, Aaron?"

He drummed his fingers against the cool fabric of the chair and after a while said levelly, "That I love you. And that I'm not quite the tyrant you think me." When he saw her eyebrows go up a fraction, he added, "Oh, I can be, I know, and I can't promise it won't happen again. But there's a reason why I acted the way I did when you turned me down——"

"I didn't turn you down."

He made a gesture of impatience. "Not in so many words, perhaps, but you weren't sure, wanted time, started worrying about your independence..."

"Is that so unreasonable?"

"Not to anyone else, perhaps. It was to me."

Emily frowned, puzzled by the harshness of his tone, the almost ruthless set to his mouth. "I don't understand," she murmured.

"No. But I hope you will."

Still that odd harshness. She lifted her chin and, looking straight at him, said, "All right, Aaron, tell me your reason, then. For being a tyrant."

He smiled, and the atmosphere lightened. "Direct and to the point as usual! That's one of the things I love about you, Green Eyes. When it's not driving me to thoughts of some rather pleasant violence."

"Aaron..." she began warningly.

"Okay," he held up a hand, "I'll get on with it."

He didn't right away, though. Instead he crossed his long legs and stared at some point high above her head. When, at last, he did speak, his voice was flat, as if he was guarding against any display of feeling or emotion.

"Emily, you have to understand that as a young man growing up in Boston I was one of the privileged. My parents were comfortably off, so I didn't want for anything—and that usually included girls. The ones I couldn't collect were the ones who didn't interest me any more than I interested them. I was young, carefree, a bit wild—and a source of great anxiety to my parents. They wanted me to go to college, so I did eventually, when they threatened to throw me out of the house unless I settled down. I even bestirred myself to pass my courses. It seemed less of an effort than failing. Then I met Carmen."

"Your wife?"

He shook his head. "No!"

Emily flinched. The word had cracked out like a gunshot.

"No," he went on, reverting to his earlier flat intonation. "Carmen was a fellow student—brilliant, beautiful in an unorthodox sort of way, and she attracted men like moths to a flame. Which was exactly what happened to them. They got burnt."

"You included?"

"Not in the way you mean. *I* succeeded with her. We were alike in a lot of ways, and we had a wild and wonderfully passionate affair, during the course of which, unfortunately, I managed to fall in love." Aaron's cool smile held no hint of real regret. "That had never happened to me before, and I found it exhilarating and a bit frightening. For the first time in my life, I was vulnerable. So I did what most besotted young men do at that age——"

"How old were you?"

"Twenty-two."

She nodded understandingly. "So you asked her to marry you, of course."

"Of course." He gave her a cool smile, and rested an ankle carelessly on his knee. "And she refused me."

Emily lowered her eyelids so that she could study his face without being too obvious about it, but she failed to detect even a flicker of emotion.

"So was that the end of the affair?" she asked cautiously, reflecting that she too had refused him.

"No. We went on seeing each other. And then after a few weeks she told me she was leaving the college, moving to another state. I was beside myself, my infatuation fueled, no doubt, by the fact that for once I wasn't getting my own way. I asked her to reconsider, to marry me instead of going away. But she wouldn't. She said her independence was too important to her and that she didn't mean to marry any man. She'd always been a free spirit, it was part of her attraction." He shrugged. "In the end I had to accept her decision."

"That must have been very painful for you," said Emily, not seeing where this chronicle of Aaron's youthful indiscretions was leading, but feeling for him just the same. He was hiding his feelings very successfully, but she knew what it was like to lose the one you loved.

"Yes, it was painful," he replied, sounding as if he was referring to a toothache. "But it was good for me in a way, because I decided I had to get away from Boston and my anxious parents, and start to do something with my life."

"Was that when you took up prospecting?"

"It was. I'd always had a hankering for the outdoor life, and I did amazingly well at it. Staked some very lucrative claims—silver mostly—and established a reputation quite quickly. After that I had no trouble selling what I'd staked, and I was well on my way to becoming one of the most successful prospectors in the Southwest. Then a letter from Carmen's parents caught up with me. I remember I was sitting in some little hole-in-the-wall café in a small town in Colorado where I'd gone to pick up supplies. There were four flies buzzing around a dirty lamp shade shaped like a shell. I hadn't bothered to read the letter till then."

Emily lifted her head sharply. His voice wasn't quite so flat now, and she sensed that the mask of cool indifference was about to crack.

"What was in the letter?" she prompted him, when after several seconds he gave no indication that he meant to go on with his story.

Aaron passed a hand over his eyes, and looked at her with a kind of frowning surprise, as if he had almost forgotten she was there. "What was in it?" he repeated bleakly. "Only the information that Carmen had been hit crossing the street, and that just before she died she told her parents that I was the father of her two-and-a-half-year-old daughter. Apparently she'd always refused to tell them my name before." He was making no attempt now to hide his bitterness. His mouth was a flat, forbidding line, and his voice rasped with remembered pain.

"Oh, dear heaven!" whispered Emily, wanting desperately to go to him, to put her arms around him and hold him, but knowing he would rebuff her if she did. "Did...? Does Tommy know?"

"She does now. I told her recently, before someone else got to her first." He gave a derisive snort. "She seemed to find it more romantic than shocking."

"Oh." Emily was at a loss for words. "What—what did...?"

"What did I do? When I read the letter?" Aaron laughed, and the sound sent a chill up her spine. "What in hell could I do? I got drunk. Didn't sober up for five days."

Emily nodded, thinking that was more than understandable. Not only had he lost the woman he probably still had some feeling for, he'd discovered he had a child he'd never met. It was enough to make anyone go off the rails. But, knowing Aaron, he'd have pulled himself up short sooner than most. Yes, she remembered now. He'd once said something about wanting to run away. And not doing it...

"And when you did sober up?" she asked quietly. "What did you do then?"

"I packed my things and went to see my daughter."

"Were—were you pleased about being a father? Once you got over the shock, I mean?"

"No, I was not pleased. I was twenty-six years old, just getting started in a job I loved, and doing damn well at it, and suddenly I was responsible for a child. Why, in heaven's name, would I be pleased?" He was looking at her with such blazing scorn now that Emily couldn't bear it. She understood his bitterness, but it still hurt.

"I'm sorry," she said softly, turning away from the suffering in his eyes. "It was a stupid question."

"Emily." His voice was unsteady. "Emily, please. Forgive me, I don't mean to take it out on you. But even now, after nearly ten years, it's hard to think of that time without wanting to break something—or somebody. I'd have been more than willing to marry Carmen if she'd given me a chance. If she'd told me about the baby..." He closed his eyes for a second. "If she'd told me about the baby, I wouldn't have missed the first two and a half years of my daughter's life. In the end, that was what I couldn't forgive. Because of Carmen's damned mania for independence, I was deprived of those years, and there's no way I can ever get them back."

"But—but you didn't really want Tommy..."

"No, I didn't. That was before I saw her."

"Oh. You mean——"

"I mean that, even though I tried to fool myself into believing I needn't do anything, I knew quite well that in the end I'd have to. That's why I got drunk. But after that futile little rebellion, of course I packed my bags and headed east."

"Of course." Emily knew that there could never have been any real doubt that Aaron, with his unyielding sense of right and wrong, would do anything but the honorable thing.

He gave her a thin smile. "Tommy's grandparents had moved to Philadelphia. It turned out that's where Carmen had gone to have my baby. She felt safe there, unlikely to run into me, in other words."

"Did—did she tell them she was pregnant?"

"Oh, yes. Apparently she told everyone but me," he replied casually, as if he were discussing the eggs he'd had for breakfast.

Emily sighed. The mask was firmly back in place.

"Okay," she said. "So——"

"So I went to Philadelphia. And saw Tommy."

"And thought she was the most beautiful child you'd ever seen," said Emily softly.

"No, I thought she was exceptionally ugly and would probably make a lot of noise. But she was mine." His voice was flat, dry, but she was sure she detected the hint of a smile in his eyes.

"Yes, I see." She nodded doubtfully. "But surely—didn't her grandparents want to keep her?"

He shook his head impatiently. "No, they didn't. Carmen had raised Tommy on her own without any help from them, and, although they loved her, they weren't young any longer. Carmen's father had retired early so that they could travel, and they had no desire to be burdened with a child."

"I hadn't thought of that," said Emily. "So naturally they wanted you to take her."

"As the lesser of two evils, yes. It wasn't that they had much use for me. Not surprisingly, they felt that I'd ruined their brilliant daughter's chances of a brilliant career. Which wasn't true. I'd have seen that Carmen finished her education—insisted on it, in fact. But she was determined to do everything on her own, so she worked during the day in some dress shop, and studied for her degree at night. Anything to avoid a commitment to me. Or any man, I imagine," Aaron added, so dispassionately that Emily wanted to scream. "Looking back on it, I don't think she liked men much."

Emily stifled an urge to say she knew the feeling. Aaron's stoic refusal to acknowledge that this resurrection of his past was hurting him—intolerably, she suspected—made her want to take him by the shoulders and rattle his teeth.

"Did you agree to take Tommy straight away, then?" she asked neutrally. "That must have been difficult."

"It wasn't difficult, it was impossible. My parents were too ill to care for a child by then, so I left her with her maternal grandparents until I could wind up my prospecting interests. Then I took the profits I'd made, hired some staff who knew what they were doing, and started Silverstone Travel. Finally, I hired Mrs. Krowiak to look after Emily."

"And after that everything was fine?"

"More or less. Apart from occasional battles with Tommy following the inevitable grandparental visits whenever they returned from their travels."

"Battles which you won, of course. But I still think it would have been simpler just to talk to them."

"Simple, yes," he replied curtly. "But not noticeably effective. They'd lost their only child, and they tried to make up for it by spoiling Tommy. Apart from which, they could barely stand the sight of me at the best of times, and couldn't believe I had anything to say worth listening to. The trouble is, as I told you, they regard me as the cause of Carmen's downfall, and ultimately, I think, of her death. They can't, or don't want to, get over that."

"But it takes two. And it wasn't your fault." Emily couldn't believe what she was hearing.

"No. Actually I suspect Carmen wanted a child, and decided I'd do as the father. She just didn't want me around to spoil her private party, which was why she avoided telling me she was pregnant." He stood up with an abruptness that startled her, propped a foot on the magazine rack, and stared broodingly at the scuffed toe of his boot. "But her parents have never seen it that way. I can sympathize with them in a sense. They've lost their daughter and they need a scapegoat. One who's useful to them, but a scapegoat nonetheless." Aaron shrugged. "In the interests of compassion, I leave things as they are, and if I have to cope with the odd tantrum—well, so be it."

Emily stared at him, her heart twisting. There was strength and resolution in the hard line of his jaw, but his eyes were hooded, deeply weary, and she knew that Aaron's coping had had its cost. The young man he had been had seen so many dreams destroyed, yet he still considered the feelings of people who disliked him. And on top of that to be blamed...

She rose to her feet instinctively, wanting to give comfort, but as she moved toward him he turned his back. She hesitated then, but only for a moment because she couldn't bear to watch his lonely reticence any longer. Biting her lip, she took a firm step forward, put her arms around his waist and rested her cheek on his bowed shoulder. She could feel him fighting to control his breathing through the dark blue material of his shirt.

"I think I understand why you couldn't bring yourself to talk to me about Carmen and her family," she said quietly. "But I'm glad you've told me now, Aaron. I—I know it must have torn you to pieces over the years..."

"At times," he replied briefly. Then after a pause, he went on in a curiously gruff voice, "But at least Tommy's not much of a problem now. She's grown and matured a lot in the past month or so, and is even showing signs of becoming passably attractive. She'll never be a raving beauty, but the ugly duckling may eventually become something of a swan. That's done wonders for her disposition, as you can imagine—and, although we did have one almighty battle when I made her leave *you*, usually we manage to avoid the old sulks and histrionics. Which is a great deal easier on us both. Even her allergies are clearing up, I'm happy to say. And there's another thing..." He turned within the circle of her arms and dropped his hands on to her shoulders. "I'm hoping that soon my daughter will have a mother—and one day maybe even a baby sister or brother."

Emily fixed her eyes just above his collarbone. She could see the sinews move in his throat. "Why haven't you married before this, Aaron?" she asked slowly. "Twelve years is a long time..."

"To go without a woman? Yes, it is. I didn't go without, exactly, but there weren't many. I was reluctant to get involved again after Carmen. But as to why it took this long..." he cupped his hands round her cheeks and smiled tenderly "...the truth is, I never found the right woman. I must have been waiting for you."

To her consternation, Emily found herself blinking back tears. Aaron was looking at her with so much love in his eyes that she thought if the floor were to open this minute and swallow her she would die happy. Then she forced herself to concentrate on reality. The floor wasn't going to open and there were still things she didn't understand...

"Aaron," she said, running her hands over the dark stubble covering his face. "Aaron, if you were waiting for me, why *wouldn't* you wait for me? When I asked you for time..."

"Ah, yes." He coiled his fingers in the hair at the back of her neck. "That's what I've been trying to tell you, Green Eyes. You see, because of everything that happened in the past, I've learned to be wary of women who insist on their independence. No, don't get me wrong," he added, as she opened her mouth. "I'm all for women doing whatever they want to do, and I haven't the slightest desire to make your decisions for you." He grinned for what seemed like the first time in eons. "Well, only some of them. And I understood your guilt over David, your fear of getting hurt again. Because I had to get over guilt too. Guilt that I'd missed the first years of Tommy's life, for which, intellectually, I know I was no more responsible than you were for David's dying. And I too was reluctant to love again for a long time. But I did—I do—love you, Emily, and when you said you couldn't marry me, after I asked you that second time——"

"As I recall, you didn't ask, you demanded," she corrected him dryly.

He bent down and kissed the tip of her nose. "So I did—for all the good it did me. But I'm afraid your friend Hatton got my goat. In any case, when you turned me down the second time, with all that rubbish about independence——"

"It's not rubbish!"

"Yes, it is. I don't want a caged bird, Emily, whatever crazy impression you may have got. But at that point I thought you were going to turn into another Carmen. A kinder version of her, of course, but still a woman who would run away from me the moment she felt her independence was threatened. Which was bound to happen sooner or later. There are some decisions that married people can't make alone."

"So that's why you left," she whispered.

"But I'd done a lot of thinking by the time I got your letter. I decided I had to see you again, to see if there might be a chance for us after all. And I came to the realization that I hadn't played fair with you, expecting you to trust me when I'd told you nothing—or next to nothing—about my past. Emily..." His jaw clenched, and she felt his fingers tighten in her hair. "Emily, when I made you tell me about David I said you had to face your memories if they weren't to destroy you. Well, I faced mine and they didn't destroy me. But talking about Carmen always reminds me that if she hadn't died in all probability I'd never have known about Tommy. I've had to accept that, of course, but even after all these years it crucifies me to think how close I came to—to not having a daughter." His voice was cracked, raw. "Even so, Green Eyes, I should have told you. However much I hated the subject, I owed you that."

"It's all right," she whispered, touching her lips to his cheek.

"No, it's not all right," he growled. "No wonder you were leery of exchanging your peace and security for marriage to a man you didn't know!" He dropped his arms to her waist, and after a while went on slowly, "But it wasn't until I was alone, with only the wind and the trees for company, that I knew I owed you much more than I'd ever given."

Emily saw the haggard lines around his eyes, and wondered what he meant about wind and trees. A lump swelled in her throat. "You mean you would have come anyway? Even without my letter?" she asked.

"Sure I would. In the end."

The lump receded somewhat. "When it suited you, I suppose," she said, more sharply than she'd intended. She closed her eyes, remembering those agonising weeks she had spent waiting with such hope for a letter that hadn't come. Frowning, she pushed his hands from her waist and moved away.

But Aaron only laughed as if a weight had been lifted from his shoulders. "Put out the green fire, sweetheart. It suited me as soon as I got your letter. The truth is, I was so damned restless, and so damned bad-tempered from missing you by the time we got back to Boston, that Tommy told me she was going to stay with Margaret, and I was to take a nice holiday by myself and not come back until I was fit to live with. She was quite adamant. So I did as I was told and took off into the bush by myself. It was the only way I could conceive of to stay sane. Out there, alone, I finally started to think clearly."

Emily recognized the love and deep tenderness in his words, and the green fire faded at once. "You mean you didn't get the letter——" she began.

"Not until four days ago. I've been driving like a fiend ever since."

"Oh," she cried, "that's why you haven't shaved! You mean you haven't had any sleep since——"

"Not much."

"You must be exhausted!" Emily was horrified. "You ought to go to bed at once."

"Just what I was about to suggest," he said, grinning.

"To sleep," she insisted primly.

"I'm not that exhausted, so don't even think it." Taking her completely by surprise, he lunged across the room and scooped her over his shoulder.

As Buster wandered out from the kitchen, tail twitching and green eyes shining suspiciously, Aaron gave her an anticipatory pat on the bottom.

And after that Emily didn't think it, because she wasn't capable of thinking of anything except the hard warmth of Aaron's body as he made love to her as if it were the very first time.

Except that this time it was even better.

Emily thought she was awake, but she kept her eyes closed just to be on the safe side. Tentatively, she put out a hand. When she'd fallen asleep, her cheek had lain on the soft mat of Aaron's chest, but some time in the night they had moved apart. If it *was* night.

Her fingers came in contact with warm skin, and she smiled. It was all right to open her eyes now. Aaron was not a figment of her dreams.

The room was dark, but she had no idea what the time was, and she didn't care. Hours ago, when it was still light, they had made love until both of them, sated, had dropped off to sleep in each other's arms—and, now that she thought about it, they hadn't even bothered to eat supper. They had had a different kind of hunger to appease.

She lay there for some time, listening to Aaron's breathing, and when dawn began to touch pink fingers to the curtains he turned over and took her back in his arms.

Much later, when the crows' morning concert was at full volume, he untangled his limbs from hers, kissed her, and sat up.

"You're smiling," said Emily, gazing up at him with languid adoration. "Tommy wouldn't believe it. She says you're always horrible in the mornings."

"Does she now? But you know better, don't you?"

"Yes," sighed Emily. "You're—inspired in the mornings."

"And you're the inspiration," he said huskily, his eyes like velvet shadows in the dawn. They were fixed on her with shattering intensity. "Emily...?"

"Mmm?"

"Emily, do you think you could possibly sit up? There's something I want to ask you."

"I can hear you from here," she said lazily.

"Maybe so, but, on a very temporary basis, I don't happen to want you just there."

Emily eyed him with a feeling of alarm. What question could possibly be so serious that he couldn't ask it unless she sat up? But she was given no chance to ponder the answer to that, because Aaron, tired of waiting, swooped down, grabbed her under the arms and hauled her upright.

"There," he said, propping the pillows at her back and pulling the sheets decorously up to her neck. "Now that you're decent and, I hope, fully awake, perhaps we can get on with a small matter I should have attended to long ago."

"What's that?" asked Emily, frowning, and not sure she wanted to hear.

His smile was tender and his voice deeply sincere, so that in the end it was his eyes that gave him away as he picked up her hand and began to speak. He couldn't quite hide the laughter lurking behind them.

"Emily," he said, "I've proposed to you on two separate occasions and made a thoroughly bad job of it, partly because I haven't had much practice, but mainly because I couldn't bear to think you might turn me down. So, on the principle that the third time's supposed to be lucky, I'll try again." He cleared his throat. "I love you, I worship you, and I don't think I can live without you. I can, on the other hand, live without your cooking. But as I fear that's not an option, I'll accept my fate. Emily Rogers—darling, adorable, contrary Emily Rogers—for the third and last time, please, will you be my wife?" When she didn't answer him at once, he added fiercely, "And if you say no again, it will give me great pleasure to give my less gentlemanly instincts full rein—although I may later plead justifiable madness."

"That," said Emily severely, "was just as bad as your other two proposals. Worse, in fact."

"I suppose it was," he admitted, attempting to look contrite and not succeeding. "All the same, if you don't hurry up and say yes, I promise you I'll——"

"Yes," said Emily.

"Kiss you," he finished. And did.

"Aaron," murmured Emily, a few hours later, as they sat at the kitchen table drinking coffee and basking in the afterglow of love, "I think we still have a few problems that need sorting out."

"Yes," he agreed. "Your cooking, for one thing. I'm damned if I'm living on a steady diet of tofu and refried beans."

"That wasn't what I was thinking of," said Emily with a sniff. "But if you must be difficult, I suppose we can take turns with the cooking. You starve one day, I'll starve the next."

He shuddered. "Is that your idea of the gentle art of compromise? Suppose we look for some common ground?"

"You mean you'd eat lentils?"

"No, I've got another idea," he said dryly. "Mrs. Krowiak has a bad knee, so she's retiring. I suggest we hire a new cook who's clever enough to keep both of us happy."

Emily laughed and relaxed. "She'd need to be some kind of genius, though, wouldn't she?"

"I don't think so. I'd just have to keep your mind off food." He smiled suggestively.

"How?" asked Emily, with feigned innocence.

"By buying you jewelry?" he suggested, with equal innocence. "Will that do?"

She shook her head.

"Fur coats?"

She glared at him, and he made a face and said hastily, "Right. Wrong, I mean. You don't do fur, do you? Okay, that leaves only one alternative."

"I was hoping you'd get around to that." She batted her eyelids seductively.

Aaron leaned across the table. "Keep that up, young lady, and we'll never get around to your problems."

"What problems?" she asked blankly. And then, remembering, "Oh, *those* problems." She sighed. "Yes, well, the thing is—where are we going to live? After we're married?"

"Do you want to stay here?"

She glanced at him with quick suspicion, but it was a question, not an objection.

"No," she said slowly, after a short pause, "I don't think I do particularly. Cinnamon Bay was my hiding place. But I don't want to hide any more."

It's true, she thought, with delight and amazement. She gave him a beaming smile.

He nodded, returning the smile with interest. "That's settled, then. We'll live in Boston and bring Tommy up here to visit every summer."

"Yes, and we'll get married at Christmas," said Emily, deciding it was time she took control of this discussion that she had initiated.

"Christmas? But that's nearly six weeks away," protested Aaron, reminding her forcibly of a small boy to whom six weeks could seem like a life sentence.

"So it is," she agreed blandly. "That will give me time to get organized, and time to calm my mother down, and it'll be the holidays by then, so you can bring Tommy up here for the wedding. She'll like Cinnamon Bay in the winter."

"And I suppose those two furry freeloaders will like Boston in the spring," he growled, fixing a jaundiced eye on Buster and Biscuit, who were curled up together on the mat.

"I'm sure they will," Emily agreed airily.

"Hmm," he grunted. "Listen, Green Eyes, if you think you're going to turn into one of those bossy, managerial women on me——"

"What will you do?" asked Emily sweetly.

His eyes glittered. "You really want to know?"

"I think I do."

She put down her coffee cup and raised her eyebrows in a provocative arch. At once Aaron rose to the bait, as well as from his chair, and without further ado he picked her up and carried her into the bedroom.

"Aaron," she murmured pensively, as he stretched himself beside her on the bed and leaned over to blow gently into her ear. "Aaron, do you think I should wear a blue dress or a green dress to our wedding?"

"No," he said, easing her head onto his shoulder.

"Or maybe yellow..."

"Green Eyes, can we talk about it later?"

"Then of course there's always ivory..."

Aaron made a sound that was a bit like an enraged bull trying to muffle a roar. "There is also the fact that if you don't stop babbling, and get down to the business in hand..." His palm covered her mouth, and he whispered a word in her ear.

Emily got down to the business.

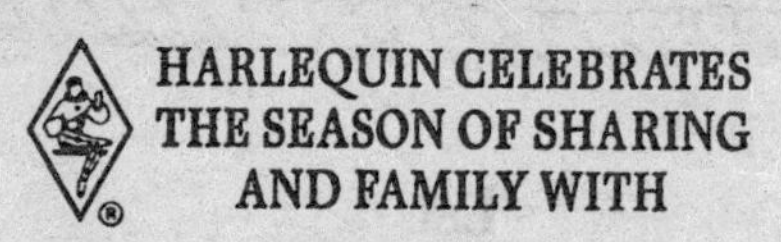

Harlequin introduces the latest member in its family of seasonal collections. Following in the footsteps of the popular *My Valentine, Just Married* and *Harlequin Historical Christmas Stories,* we are proud to present FRIENDS, FAMILIES, LOVERS. A collection of three new contemporary romance stories about America at its best, about welcoming others into the circle of love.... Stories to warm your heart...

By three leading romance authors:

KATHLEEN EAGLE
SANDRA KITT
RUTH JEAN DALE

Available in October, wherever Harlequin books are sold.

THANKS

HARLEQUIN ROMANCE®